SECRET OF THE
Unicorn  Queen

THE
OF THE

"Out of the corner of her eye, she saw Dr. Reit's panic-stricken face as he leaped forward. For an instant his hand closed about her wrist. But before he could pull her free, an unearthly wind seized her. Sheila screamed as she was dragged away from Dr. Reit—

Then she was tumbling helplessly down and down into a dizzying world of stormy blue . . ."

* * *

And so begins Sheila McCarthy's incredible journey to the mysterious and magical world of Arren—a whole dimension away from home! Join her as she meets a beautiful, silver-haired Unicorn Queen, a handsome boy warrior who battles for good in an evil-torn land, a dark wizard who vows to capture Sheila, a gentle unicorn named Morning Star, and magical creatures, both good and bad, as you share . . .

THE SECRET OF THE UNICORN QUEEN
SUN BLIND

Will Sheila ever find her way back home?

THE SECRET OF THE Unicorn Queen

❧ BOOK TWO ❧

Sun Blind

GWEN HANSEN

FAWCETT COLUMBINE ❖ GIRLS ONLY
NEW YORK

With thanks to Suzanne Weyn and
Stephanie St. Pierre

RLI: $\dfrac{\text{VL6 + up}}{\text{IL7 + up}}$

A Fawcett Columbine Book
Published by Ballantine Books
Copyright © 1988 by Parachute Press, Inc.

Library of Congress Catalog Card Number: 87-91872

ISBN: 0-449-90297-8

Cover design by Dale Fiorillo
Illustration by Rowena Morrill

Manufactured in the United States of America
First Edition: November 1988
10 9 8 7 6 5 4 3 2 1

SECRET THE OF THE
Unicorn Queen

⚹ BOOK TWO ⚹

Sun Blind

1

❧❖❧
Hunted

Someone shook Sheila McCarthy roughly from her sleep. "Wake up, we're moving out!"

With a groan, Sheila turned over and tried to burrow beneath the thin wool cloth that covered her. A moment later the blanket was pulled off and strong arms grabbed her, lifting her into a sitting position.

The dark-haired boy who held her spoke in a quiet, urgent voice. "Nanine has seen Dynasian's men in the village. We can't stay here any longer. We're breaking camp now."

"Where are we going?" Sheila mumbled, trying not to sound as groggy as she felt.

Darian sounded weary when he answered. "South, to Ansar, I think. I just wish that for once we could do this during the day."

"It'd be a change," Sheila agreed. In the month since she had been riding with Illyria, the Unicorn Queen, she had lost count of the number of times she had been wakened in the middle of the night to flee the tyrant Dynasian's soldiers. "All right," she said, as the familiar sense of danger set in, "I'm awake."

In spite of the situation Darian sounded amused.

3

"Well, then, stop looking so sleepy." He released her and stood up. "Get your things together and be ready to ride."

"I'll be ready in a minute," Sheila promised, but Darian had already moved on and was kneeling by the fire, gathering a battered assortment of copper pots and cooking utensils.

Sheila shivered in the cold night air and drew her worn blue tunic more tightly around her. She had arrived in this world wearing jeans and a shirt. Now the jeans were frayed cutoffs and her shirt, torn in a scuffle in the city of Campora, had been replaced by one of Darian's old tunics. It was big on her (Darian had almost collapsed laughing when she first tried it on and it fell to her knees) and needed mending, but it was woven of a soft, warm material. She adjusted the tunic, fastened a leather belt around her waist, and slipped a light sword into the sheath that hung from it.

Automatically she rolled up the wool blanket and began to scatter the pile of leaves she had used as a pillow. For the thousandth time she asked herself how she, a completely normal fourteen-year-old girl from the twentieth century, had wound up in this strange world of unicorns and warriors. *You fell into Dr. Reit's time machine, that's how,* she answered herself irritably, unable to stop the familiar wave of homesickness. No matter what adventures she had in this world, it seemed she always longed to return to her own. How could she forget her family and friends? And how could she let herself face the truth: unless Dr. Reit found a way to get her back to her world, she would never see any of them again. *So stop worrying over something you can't change,* she told herself. *There are more important things to deal with right now.*

Breaking camp meant leaving no trace that the unicorn riders had ever been in this place. On the night that Illyria and her warriors had freed the unicorns that Dynasian held captive, the tyrant had set a price on their heads. Sheila, who in her own time had never done anything more criminal than cut study hall, was now an official "enemy of the empire." If it weren't so real, it would be funny.

She used her hands to rake through the grass so there was no longer an imprint where she had lain. Around her, by the light of the dying fire, she could see the other riders working swiftly. And in the distance she could hear the soft, impatient whinnying of the unicorns. The animals knew they were moving out. They always knew.

Quickly Sheila gathered up the wool blanket and grabbed for the two things that had become her constant companions. The first, a light wooden spear with an iron tip, was from the world of the Unicorn Queen. The second item came from her own world. It was a simple green nylon backpack, filled with things that were ordinary in her own time—a tape player, a flashlight, a mirror, some bubble gum—but were considered "magic" here. Even among the riders of the Unicorn Queen there were some who still called her "sorceress" because of the backpack.

Stuffing her blanket into the pack, Sheila crossed the wooded camp. The moon was only about half full, but the night was clear and the stars shone like a white swath across the sky. Though Sheila hadn't trained herself to move through the darkness the way Illyria's warriors had, she could see fairly well. That, of course, meant that Dynasian's men would also be able to see without trouble. It was a good night to hunt fugitives.

"Where's your saddle?" demanded a girl, coming up behind Sheila.

"Hidden with the others." Sheila tried to keep her voice calm. She was already feeling panicky at the thought of Dynasian's soldiers closing in on them. The last thing she needed was an argument with Dian.

"Well, find it, then, and stop standing around!" Dian ordered. Sixteen years old and the second youngest in Illyria's band, Dian had been resentful of Sheila from the start. "Dynasian's men will probably be here by the time you finally locate your saddle," she went on. "Do you think we have all night to wait for you?"

"I wasn't standing around—" Sheila began indignantly.

"Hush, both of you!" Myno, Illyria's lieutenant, clamped a powerful hand on each girl's shoulder and spoke in a fierce, low tone. "This is no time for arguing, and if either one of you lives till tomorrow, I swear I'll have your hides for it. Now, you know what you have to do. Don't make me speak to you again."

Both girls mumbled apologies, and Myno released them with a rough shake.

Sheila glared at Dian. Even when they were running for their lives, Dian managed to find a way to get her in trouble.

"You've done it now," Darian said matter-of-factly. He held out the worn leather saddle that Sheila had used ever since the unicorn Morning Star had accepted her as its rider. "I'd rather face Dynasian himself than an angry Myno."

Sheila took the saddle from him with a sigh. She was never sure whether Darian, Illyria's handsome sixteen-year-old brother, was the most intriguing boy she had ever met or the most irritating. Sometimes he had an absolute talent for saying the thing she least wanted to hear.

"Don't worry," he assured her, and she couldn't tell

if he was teasing or not. "Illyria's never let Myno kill one of her riders."

Darian led the way into the sheltered glade where the others waited. As always, Sheila's breath caught at the sight of the warriors. In the center of the clearing, Illyria, her long silver-blond hair half-caught in thick braids, sat tall and regal on the magnificent Quiet Storm. Quiet Storm had been the first unicorn to appear in Illyria's homeland. Now his silver coat and horn shone in the starlight, as if he were somehow part of it—a creature spun out of stars and moon.

On Illyria's right, Myno, her sword drawn, sat astride a palomino unicorn. On her left was Kara, the archer, on a dark brown unicorn with a white star across his forehead. Behind them Sheila saw the other riders: Pelu, the healer; Nanine, the regal black princess who had rebelled and fled her own court; and Dian. A small herd of wild unicorns who ran with Illyria's warriors moved restlessly among the mounted riders. All of the unicorns and riders looked very beautiful—and very deadly.

Illyria watched, her gaze calm, as Sheila and Darian joined them. A month ago, when Sheila had first stumbled through Dr. Reit's time machine into this parallel universe, she hadn't even known the front end of a saddle from the back. Now her hands worked deftly to slip the saddle over Morning Star's back and fasten the soft girth around the animal's stomach. In one smooth movement she lifted herself onto the unicorn's back and ran a hand through Morning Star's silky black mane. Then, with her free hand, she reached for the spear she had set in the ground. Beside her Darian and Dian drew their own spears. At Illyria's signal the small band of warriors raised their weapons in a brief salute, then followed the unicorn queen into the night.

Illyria always chose her course carefully, and now she led her band along a tangled path of narrow back roads that wound south. They were riding inland, far from the busy ports and towns along the coast. Sheila guessed that their route to Ansar would probably take twice as long as the main roads. Then again, if they followed the main roads, they probably wouldn't survive the night. Dynasian's men seemed to own the coast.

The cool night wind rushed through Sheila's hair as the road widened and the unicorns broke into a full gallop, their hoofs barely touching the ground. They were impossibly light when they ran, and Sheila sometimes thought if they could only go a little faster, they would be flying. Her pack bounced gently against her back, and she leaned forward in the saddle, winding her left hand more tightly through Morning Star's mane. Although unicorns accepted saddles, they were far too wild to let anyone fit them with bridle or bit. Like the other riders, Sheila had learned to hold on to the thick, silky mane with one hand and carry her spear in the other. She still considered it a miracle that she managed to stay on at all, and suspected that most of the credit belonged to Morning Star.

The land rose up in a series of low hills, and the road narrowed again. At a signal from Illyria the unicorns slowed to a canter, and the riders fell in two by two. Sheila found Darian, who had been riding ahead near Illyria, at her side.

"Any sign of Dynasian's men?" she asked.

Darian shook his head. "Not yet. Which doesn't mean they haven't set a trap for us ahead. And if they have, we'll all ride straight into it. I don't know why we don't split up."

"Did you suggest it to Illyria?"

"Every time we go through this," he said, barely concealing his impatience. "I've told her I'm willing to go ahead as a scout, and that we should move in at least two groups. But my sister doesn't believe in splitting up her warriors when we're being pursued."

"Well," Sheila said uncertainly, "I'm sure Illyria has her reasons. I don't think I'd want to face a band of Dynasian's men without the others there. I mean, there aren't that many of us. Even when we're all together, there's a good chance we'll be outnumbered by the soldiers."

"Exactly," Darian said.

"What?"

Darian had the maddening habit of twisting her words around so it sounded as if she were arguing on his side. "We're going to be outnumbered anyway," he said logically, "so why give them the chance to finish us all off at once?"

"We're not giving anyone a chance to finish us off," said a very firm voice behind him. Illyria, whom Sheila could have sworn was riding at the head of the band, drew Quiet Storm even with Darian's unicorn and stared down at her dark-haired brother. "And when I need advice from a sixteen-year-old cub," she continued in a cold voice, "I'll ask for it. Let it go, Darian."

Darian said nothing but glared back, looking at that moment very much like his sister.

There was a moment of tense silence.

"That wasn't fair," Illyria admitted softly. "You've proven yourself a warrior. I shouldn't have called you a—"

"I'm sorry, too," Darian broke in. He shrugged apologetically. "It's just that I can't even look at a tree anymore without wondering if one of Dynasian's soldiers is hiding behind it."

"You, too?" Sheila looked at him in amazement. She

had been positive she was the only one who was so paranoid. Sure that Dian would laugh her out of the camp, she hadn't dared tell anyone how nervous this whole "enemy of the state" business was making her.

"And me," Illyria confessed with a grin. "I'm tired of being hunted, which is why we ride to Ansar. Dynasian holds a fortress there. It's time I brought the hunt home to the hunter's door." Then, without another word, the Unicorn Queen pressed her heels into Quiet Storm and rode on ahead.

Sheila had no idea how long they had been riding. Ever since she had given her watch to Darian, she had been a little fuzzy on time. What had ever made her believe that, like the other riders, she would learn to tell the time from the positions of the sun and stars? Basically, she was only good at recognizing dawn, noon, and sunset, and on overcast days she lost noon altogether.

Now the night sky was turning a charcoal gray, and the road was becoming steeper. They were entering the southern mountains, an area known for its hot, dry lands. The trees along the side of the road were thinning already. There had been no sign of Dynasian's men, and the riders' careful pace on the narrow road was deceptively calm. Tired, Sheila let herself be rocked by Morning Star's gentle rhythm, almost forgetting that they were being pursued.

"No sleeping in the saddle!" called a teasing voice.

Sheila sat up with a start to find Pelu riding beside her. "Do you think we'll reach Ansar by dawn?" Sheila asked.

"Not unless it moves itself north. We're a good five days away from the city—and Dynasian's fortress."

"Oh," Sheila said, though what she really wanted to say was that she was very relieved. She had met Dynasian once before, and what she had seen in his eyes had terrified her. She wasn't exactly looking forward to riding straight into his stronghold.

She couldn't help glancing at Pelu to see if she felt the same way. Pelu looked inexplicably happy.

"What is it?" Sheila asked, puzzled.

Pelu pointed overhead. At first Sheila didn't see anything. The sun had barely started its ascent and the sky was still dark, but as she looked harder she saw deep shadows against the grayness—shadows of birds as large as men.

"The eagles," Sheila said in awe. "They're back!"

Pelu nodded, smiling as the harsh cries of the birds began to fill the air. "Illyria will be pleased," she said in a dreamy voice.

"And you?" Sheila teased.

Pelu blushed, answering her question.

"You fell in love with one of Laric's men?" Sheila said, eager for details.

"Hush!" Pelu's fair skin reddened. "Eagles have a very keen sense of hearing. They can probably hear every word we say."

"I don't believe this," Sheila muttered. Only in this world did someone have to worry about her boyfriend overhearing her because he happened to be transformed into an eagle and was presently flying overhead.

Everyone knew eagles didn't fly in flocks, and everyone knew that they didn't grow to the size of men, but the birds who flew overhead *were* men, enspelled by Mardock, Dynasian's evil sorcerer. In their human form the eagles were a warrior band led by Laric, prince of Perian, Illyria's love. Long ago Laric had angered Dynasian. The result was Mardock's curse: Except for five days and nights of the full moon, Laric and his men were condemned to roam the skies as eagles.

"Of all the things Mardock could have done, why did he curse them *this* way?" Sheila wondered aloud.

Pelu shrugged. "There are two things that matter to Prince Laric—stopping Dynasian and being with Illyria. Mardock's curse ensures that he has little chance of doing either."

"Then why does Mardock let them become men again under the full moon?"

"Let them?" Pelu gave an uncharacteristically bitter laugh. "He could not help it. Mardock's powers are weakest under the full moon, and fortunately, it is under the moon that the powers of Perian are strongest."

Sheila had never been clear about Perian. All she knew was that it was another country, entirely outside Dynasian's empire. And it was a magical land. She didn't know what sort of powers Laric and his men might have, but Laric had given Illyria Quiet Storm, and there was no doubt that the unicorns were magical creatures.

"Do you remember Cam?" Pelu asked, breaking into her thoughts.

Sheila thought back to the night Laric's men had arrived in the nick of time to help the riders steal one of Dynasian's ships and escape from Campora with half the captive unicorns aboard. At first she couldn't tell one warrior from another. They all looked strong and tall and incredibly fierce. But she remembered Cam. He was fair-haired, like Pelu, and had a warm, easy manner.

"Is he the one you like?" she asked Pelu.

The healer nodded.

"In Perian his family breeds horses. He says when we have defeated Dynasian, he would like me to visit."

It was perfect, Sheila thought. Pelu, who loved animals nearly as much as she loved her own life, falling in love with a man who bred horses.

Overhead the eagles wheeled against the sky, following the unicorns below. One of the golden birds called out in what sounded like harsh, angry protest.

"Oh, Sheila," Pelu said wistfully, "Mardock's curse is hard on them all. We cannot let Dynasian win."

Dawn had just broken, hotter than any dawn Sheila could remember. The sun was barely on the horizon, and already it felt as if it was ninety degrees. Pelu insisted that the riders stop often to give the unicorns water, and though they all carried leather water flasks, everyone knew that the supply wouldn't last long. Myno had even suggested to Illyria that perhaps there was another route they could take—one in which they would not all die of thirst. But Illyria had just frowned and said that they were going exactly as they should.

They were climbing higher and higher into a brown, dry landscape. In her own world Sheila's family had driven west one summer, and what she saw now reminded her of the mountains of northern New Mexico, except that in New Mexico the mountains had been covered with aspen and evergreen. Here there was no greenery at all. Everything looked as if the color had been baked right out of it.

The strange thing was that the higher they climbed and the more remote the land became, the more roads there were. The narrow road they were on branched and branched again, was crossed half a dozen times, and at one point seemed to lead in at least five different directions. They didn't see any houses. They didn't see any people. Never hesitating, Illyria led them as if she had memorized the way.

"What are all these roads for?" Sheila asked when she and Darian were riding alongside each other again.

"You mean *who* are all these roads for?" There was a wariness in his voice that made Sheila uneasy.

"Who, what . . . you know what I mean. There isn't anything up here."

"No," Darian replied thoughtfully. "But let's say all this land was yours, and you wanted to make sure that if you had to, you could get around it easily. You'd make sure there were roads."

"Not me. If I had the money to buy this much land, you can bet I'd spend it on some fancy villa overlooking the sea. Who in their right mind would buy all this desert and then carve roads into it? Even the unicorns have trouble in these mountains."

"He may not be in his right mind," Darian answered, "and I don't think he had to *buy* the land."

Despite the heat, Sheila felt a chill run through her as the meaning of Darian's words became clear. "What you mean," she said slowly, "is that we're in Dynasian's territory."

Morning Star's shrill whinny—a sound Sheila had come to recognize as the unicorn's warning of certain danger—was her answer.

2

❧ ❖ ❧

A Battle and a Barn

Morning Star's warning was answered at once by the low, clear call of Illyria's battle cry. Sheila's grip on her spear tightened, and her heart began to pound as Myno drew her sword and gave the signal to fight. *Fight who?* Sheila wondered. The only people in sight were the unicorn riders, all of them holding their weapons ready. The unicorns were completely still, poised for action at a split second.

The silence seemed endless. Then suddenly, from behind, came the sound of thundering hoofbeats. Dynasian's soldiers were upon them.

Despite the heat, the tyrant's men wore thick leather armor and helmets with a narrow strip that went down the nose. There was something very sinister about them, and Sheila shuddered as she realized what it was—the helmets made the soldiers look like executioners.

Their leader, a broad man with heavily muscled arms, sent his spear flying. There was a reassuring *thunk* as the spear connected with Myno's shield, and Myno's voice rose above the noise of the horses and the men. "Now," she cried, "*we* attack!"

Fearlessly Dian aimed her spear and hit a burly, bearded

soldier. Darian, Nanine, and Pelu joined the attack, swords flying.

Sheila sat on Morning Star, paralyzed. A heavyset soldier aimed a spear at her, and instinctively she ducked, flattening herself against the unicorn's back. Another soldier, on foot, ran toward Morning Star's side. With a rising sense of terror, Sheila realized the soldier was going to pull her off the unicorn. She heard Myno's endless drills running through her head: "Give the enemy the spear or give him the blade, but don't give him a chance." Still, throwing a spear at a target was very different from throwing it at a man.

Sheila took a deep breath, aimed at the soldier who was charging her, and forced herself to throw. She was incredibly relieved when the spear sailed over his head. But her relief vanished as she realized that the only weapon she had left was her sword. She drew it from its sheath at her waist and prayed she wouldn't have to use it.

Time seemed to slow as she waited for the soldier to make his move, and Sheila wondered frantically if she would actually be able to use the blade.

She never had the chance to find out. Morning Star darted to the side of the road and reared up on her hind legs, sending her rider flying. Sheila landed hard on her backside. She wasn't sure what was worse—the jolt or the shock of Morning Star betraying her in the middle of a battle.

It took only seconds before she realized that Morning Star had not betrayed her. Rather, the unicorn had acted to get her out of harm's way. Now it was Morning Star who was doing the fighting, and the unicorn on her own was far more dangerous than she was with Sheila on her back. Morning Star made straight for the soldier who had come at Sheila. He swung his sword in a low arc, trying to cut the animal at the knees.

"*Stop!*" Sheila screamed, desperately trying to warn the man.

It was no use. Before his sword had completed its arc, Morning Star's horn had pierced his armor, lifted him into the air, and dropped him in a limp heap. Having dispatched that attacker, the unicorn eagerly sought the next enemy. Sheila had to look away as the unicorn tore into another soldier. She stood shakily, willing herself to go back into the battle, but her knees gave way, and she sat back down.

All around Sheila the unicorns and their riders were doing a thorough job of defeating the small troop of soldiers. Quiet Storm and Illyria plowed through a crescent of five archers who never even loosed their arrows. Myno rode her palomino like an avenging demon. Sheila could barely tell the unicorn's horn from Myno's sword; both were covered in blood. And Darian—he no longer seemed a teenage boy but a brave warrior, crossing swords with a soldier twice his size. From the movements of Dynasian's man, Sheila knew what the outcome would be. The soldier was obviously stronger, but Darian was little and quick and had unerring aim. His blade found its way home easily.

As the battle raged on, Sheila was sick.

It seemed like hours later that Illyria knelt by Sheila's side, offering her a leather flask filled with water. Illyria's silver braids were almost completely undone, and her face was grimy with dust and sweat. Her tunic, always ragged, looked even worse than usual.

"Is everyone all right?" Sheila asked as she gave back the flask.

"There are enough cuts and bruises to keep Pelu busy for a while, but we were lucky. No one was hurt badly. How are you?"

Sheila couldn't keep the bitterness out of her voice. "Great, for someone who fell off her unicorn and got sick to her stomach."

"You could not have fallen off if Morning Star had not deemed it best," Illyria said gently. "Of the two of you, she is the more experienced fighter, and you must trust her judgment."

"You mean," Sheila said, "of the two of us, she is the *only* fighter. . . . I'm sorry."

"There's nothing to be sorry for. You fought by my side in Campora," Illyria reminded her. "But that was a different kind of fight." A smile played at the corner of the Unicorn Queen's mouth. "If you promise not to tell, I'll let you in on a secret."

Sheila nodded.

"Swear," Illyria ordered with mock sternness.

"I swear. I'll never tell."

"Especially Darian," Illyria added with an unmistakable grin.

"Especially Darian."

"Well, then, you should know that the first year I fought I shook before and after every battle. For hours. I used to have to make up excuses to go off on my own afterward so no one would see what awful shape I was in. Myno, of course, knew exactly what was happening, but then, Myno misses very little. And she's very good at keeping secrets."

Sheila smiled, only half-believing the story. Illyria was probably just trying to cheer her up.

Illyria's blue eyes held Sheila's in an unwavering gaze. "Sheila, the taking of a man's life, even a man who fights for a tyrant, is a very serious thing. It *ought* to affect you." The unicorn queen stood up. "You come from a place and time where this sort of bloodshed is not usual for girls your age."

The understatement of the year, Sheila thought, but to Illyria she said, "Not too many of my friends back home are warriors."

Illyria shrugged. "Perhaps that is a good thing. In any case, you need not be ashamed. But now, if you're feeling better, Morning Star could use some attention. She has earned it."

Sheila took a curry brush and comb from her pack and went to attend to Morning Star. The unicorn nuzzled her gently, her nose velvety soft in Sheila's palm. "You're a lethal beast," Sheila said fondly, and then put an arm around the unicorn, hugging her. "Thanks for saving my life."

Five days later Illyria led her band to the southern coast of the empire. The dry mountains where they had fought Dynasian's soldiers had given way to hills covered with cedar, cypress, and olive trees. Even better, as far as Sheila was concerned, were the small villages that welcomed the unicorns and their riders.

Tonight they were in a place called Nolad, about a day's ride from Ansar. They hadn't planned to stop at all, but there had been a sudden downpour, and a woman named Yvere had offered to let them spend the night in her barn.

Whinnying softly, the unicorns immediately made friends with Yvere's horses, and the riders settled into the loft above the stalls. Considering that they were so close to Dynasian's stronghold, Sheila felt surprisingly content. It was good to be safe inside, listening to the rain fall on the thatched roof.

"This is luxury!" exclaimed Kara, stretching out in the sweet-smelling hay.

Nanine yawned. "In my land," she said, "this is not what we call luxury."

"What do you expect when you grow up in a palace?" Darian asked. Absently he toyed with the bandage that had covered his right wrist ever since the battle. He grinned at Nanine. "I told you you were spoiled."

"At least I grew up," Nanine retorted. Her golden necklace, inlaid with turquoise and coral, gleamed in the light of the barn's oil lamp. Even in a worn tunic covered with bits of straw, Nanine looked every inch the princess.

Sheila looked down at her own clothing. Somehow she had managed to tear her tunic's right shoulder. Always too big, it was now threatening to slide off altogether. She tugged on it, wishing she had a few safety pins in her pack.

"Don't let it bother you," Illyria said, watching her. "We'll all have new clothing soon."

"We will?" Dian, who always tried to sound so cool, couldn't keep the excitement out of her voice.

Darian rolled his eyes.

"Tomorrow," Illyria said. "We'll make camp in the hills outside Ansar then. And we certainly can't ride into the city looking like this."

"We can't ride in at all," Darian pointed out. "Don't you think a band of warriors riding around with a herd of unicorns is just a little conspicuous?"

Illyria grinned and threw a fistful of hay at her brother. "Your faith in me is overwhelming. When I said we'd have new clothing, I meant disguises."

There was a soft knock at the barn door, and Yvere, a small, serious woman, came in. She lifted a shawl from her head, and Sheila saw that beneath it her hair and tunic were soaked. *If only they had umbrellas in this crazy place,* Sheila thought.

"Forgive me for interrupting," Yvere began.

"You didn't interrupt anything important," Illyria assured her, giving Darian a mock glare. "Will you join us, or would you rather I came down?"

Yvere hesitated, almost as if she were afraid.

Illyria climbed down the wooden ladder and stood before their hostess. Watching them together, Sheila didn't blame Yvere for feeling timid. Illyria was a good head taller than the woman and stood straight and strong. Yvere's small frame was hunched over from years of working in the fields.

"You are going to Ansar?" Yvere asked.

Illyria nodded.

"That is good," Yvere said, with the closest she had come to a smile.

Illyria sighed. "I mean to find Dynasian's fortress. I'm not sure that's so good."

"You'll have no trouble finding his fortress," Yvere said. "But I think you will find something else of interest." Quiet Storm came up behind the woman and playfully rubbed the side of his head against her shoulder. Yvere turned and ran her hand through his mane. "Yes, that's right," she murmured. "He knows."

"Knows what?" Dian called from the loft. Illyria turned and gave Dian a severe look, and Sheila was very relieved that Dian had been the one to ask.

"Oh!" Pelu said, with a soft gasp. "She means the unicorns."

Dynasian had committed countless crimes against his people, but among the worst was capture of the unicorns. It was known throughout the empire that the unicorns were a force of Light. Where the unicorns were free, the land and people prospered. When they were taken by the tyrant, disease and famine followed. Illyria and her riders had sworn to free the unicorns, and indeed, with the help of Laric's men, had freed half of those Dynasian held in Campora. But the tyrant still held half of the herd, and now Yvere was telling them that the unicorns were in Ansar.

At least some of them. "I don't know how many there are," Yvere went on, "but there are rumors all through the city that he hides them in his fortress."

"He always keeps them well guarded," Illyria said grimly. She looked up at her small troop in the loft. "Are you ready to storm a fortress?"

"In Campora it was his palace," Myno muttered. "In Ansar it's his fortress. He's going to get to know us awfully well."

"You needn't do it alone," Yvere said. "Ansar may be filled with Dynasian's men, but it's also filled with people who hate him. He has caused endless grief in that city." She paused again to stroke Quiet Storm, and Sheila saw her face lighten as she touched the unicorn. It was almost as if she looked younger, or as if she hadn't had such a hard life. Sheila had seen it happen before—the unicorns had that effect on almost everyone.

"I've heard rumors," Illyria said. "There's a rebel group. They call themselves—"

"The Sareen," Yvere finished.

"It means . . . something like . . . Warriors of the Sun," Illyria translated for Sheila's benefit.

When Sheila had first entered this world, Pelu had touched her with a gleaming blue stone she called the Gem of Speaking. Sheila had never figured out exactly what it was or how it worked. All she knew was that it allowed her to understand the language of Illyria and the riders. Unfortunately, it didn't work with any of the other languages in the empire. Or with many of the names, which didn't have an exact translation into English.

"The Sareen are very strong," Yvere went on. "They've attacked Dynasian many times."

"Where do we find them?" Illyria asked.

Yvere gave Quiet Storm a final pat, pulled her shawl over her head, and opened the barn door. Outside, the rain was still coming down in torrents. "Oh, you won't have to find the Sareen," she answered as she let herself out. "I guarantee they'll find you."

3

Dian's Plan

Sheila slid off Morning Star's back with a grateful sigh. They had left Yvere's barn just before dawn and ridden most of the day. Illyria had led them single file down a twisting mountain road and finally through a narrow pass to this—well, the best way Sheila could describe it was a miniature canyon. Two walls of solid brown rock rose up on either side, and between them ran a clear stream bordered with willow trees and high wild grasses. In this land where everything seemed carved out of dry brown rock, it was like they had found a little paradise.

Sheila took her bedroll from the unicorn's back and then removed the saddle. At once Morning Star ran to join the others by the stream. The unicorns clearly liked this place—they were frisking in the water, prancing with delight. Sheila grinned as she watched Darian, who was walking along the bank, get thoroughly splashed.

Myno's voice cracked through the camp. "Get yourself settled quickly. And then gather at Illyria's tent."

That was a surprise. They hadn't used the tents since they had left Campora and Dynasian had declared them outlaws. The tents just took too long to take down when you had to strike camp and flee in the middle of the night.

If they were using them again, it must mean they intended to stay for a few nights and that this place was relatively safe. Sheila, of course, had not come to this world carrying her own tent, and now she wondered whom she would be rooming with.

Kara solved the problem for her. "Help me set this up," she called to Sheila, "and then you can stay with me."

For a while Sheila and Kara wrestled with cloth flaps, leather ties, and at least fifteen wooden stakes.

"If you put that stake in there," Kara said calmly, "neither one of us is going to be able to sit up. You're pulling the top down flat."

"Oh," Sheila said, studying the tent with confusion.

"Try putting it in over here," Kara offered, pointing to the obvious place to nail in the stake.

How can this be so complicated? Sheila wondered. She couldn't help thinking about her own tent at home—an aluminum and nylon domelike thing that practically put itself up.

"We're home!" Kara said when the patched little tent was finally standing. She surveyed the canyon with a warrior's critical eye. "It's not bad," she declared. "We'll only need two people on watch." She pointed to the mouth of the canyon, where they had ridden in. "Someone guarding that pass and then someone walking the perimeter of the camp, just in case."

"I think it's great," Sheila said happily. The willow trees moved gently in the breeze, and the stream looked almost silver in the late afternoon light. Three other tents had already gone up, and Dian and Darian were starting a fire for the evening meal. For the first time since leaving Campora, there was an easy, relaxed feeling in the camp.

"Kara," Sheila began curiously, "how did Illyria find

this place? The route we took—a homing pigeon would have gotten lost."

"She rides Quiet Storm," the archer answered simply. "So?"

Kara took an arrow from her quiver and ran a finger along its shaft. "All of the unicorns have powers that go beyond the ordinary. You've seen that. But even among unicorns Quiet Storm is special. Ask Illyria about him sometime."

"Whatever you want to ask will have to wait," said Myno, coming up behind them. "Illyria wants to talk strategy now—with all of you."

Sheila followed Kara and Myno to Illyria's tent, where the other riders had gathered. They were sitting on the grass in front of the tent, as ragged a bunch as ever there was. Not one of them had a tunic that wasn't ripped, patched, stained, and faded. Dian, Sheila noticed, was sitting next to Darian, and Sheila couldn't help feeling an irrational stab of jealousy.

Illyria stepped out of her tent and the riders fell quiet. It might have been a trick of the light, but the Unicorn Queen looked even more beautiful than usual. Her thick braids of silver hair seemed to catch the afternoon sun and positively glowed. Her tanned skin looked even darker.

"Yes," she began, "we've come to a very pretty place. And I think we'll be here for a few nights, at least. But we have work to do. We're less than two hours from Ansar. I've never been there, but I'm told that the city lies at the foot of the mountain that is Dynasian's fortress."

"That means," Myno broke in, "that either he or his men see everything that goes on in the city."

"We've sworn a vow to free the unicorns," Illyria went on. "If what Yvere told us is true, then our course is clear. We must find a way into the fortress and free them." She looked at her band with a wry smile. "As my brother so accurately pointed out, we're not exactly an inconspicuous bunch. If we even approach the city looking like this—or riding the unicorns—we can expect to find ourselves in Dynasian's dungeons."

"But we need to find a way into that fortress," Myno added. "And we want to make contact with the rebel forces. So we'll need disguises."

"I can fashion disguises," Nanine said, "but not out of willow leaves. I'll need two or three bolts of cloth."

"That's easy," Dian said. "I'll slip into the market-place and steal them."

"There's no need to steal," Kara said.

"You expect me to walk in looking like this and ask to buy cloth?" Dian demanded.

"She has a point," Darian said reasonably.

"There'll be no stealing," Illyria ruled. "However, Dian *does* have a point." She slipped into the tent and returned with a small leather pouch. "Here's twenty pieces of silver. I don't expect you to bargain for the cloth, but you can leave this as payment for the merchant. It will more than cover the cost."

She turned to Nanine. "Do you think you could work up something for her to wear into Ansar . . . maybe using one of the tents?"

Nanine gave a sullen nod. Tents obviously did not fit her idea of suitable fashion.

"You can use mine," Kara volunteered.

Sheila was torn between admiration for Kara's selfless-ness and being outraged at having to give up the tent they had worked so hard to assemble.

"I don't like this," Myno muttered. "It's too risky. What if she's caught? What if she gets lost?"

Dian began to sputter indignantly, but Illyria silenced

her with a look. "Dian," she said, "I know your bravery, but perhaps this is one mission you should not undertake alone."

Myno flashed the Unicorn Queen a broad grin. "And I've got the perfect partner for her," she said. "Sheila, tonight you'll let Nanine do what she can about disguising you. Tomorrow at dawn you leave for Ansar with Dian."

4

❧❖❧

In the Marketplace

Sheila tugged irritably at the thick dress that covered her. Although Nanine had done the best she could for them, both Sheila and Dian looked as if they were wearing small tents—which they were! The heavy, worn material was stiff with dust and dirt, and though Nanine had tried to make the garments shapely by adding belts, the fabric stuck out at weird angles from their bodies. Worse, the dresses, if you could call them that, were ankle length. After weeks in cutoffs and a tunic, Sheila felt as if she were walking in a bag. Also, she had grown so used to riding Morning Star that it had never even occurred to her that she and Dian would have to *walk* to Ansar.

Sheila was absolutely miserable. The sun was beating down on them, she was trapped in this horrible hot "dress," she was probably going to be arrested for stealing, and to top it all off, she was stuck with Dian.

Dian looked no happier than Sheila. And, except for growling, "You'd better not get us caught," she hadn't said a word since they left the camp. Sheila suspected that if either one of them could have figured out a way to argue with Myno, Dian would have had a different partner.

The road that led into Ansar was broader than any

road Sheila had ever seen and crowded with travelers on their way to the city markets. There were merchants driving donkeys, soldiers on their war horses, and families on foot. Animals were everywhere—goats, pigs, and dogs roamed freely, as if they were going to Ansar on their own. Sheila found herself darting out of the way of a cart loaded with chickens only to nearly collide with a woman balancing a huge basket of fruit on her shoulder. With relief, she realized that no one they had passed had given her knapsack a second look. It was just one more bundle on the way to market.

The sun was nearly overhead when Dian gasped, "There it is!"

Sheila, who had been staring at the road, wishing they had shopping malls in this place, looked up, startled.

She expected a city and what she saw was a huge wall built of thick sand-colored stones. And though the wall was high, it was completely dwarfed by the mountain that rose to the right of it. The odd thing about the mountain was that it looked as if its top was completely level. It figured that Dynasian would level a mountain for his own purposes.

"The city's inside the wall?" Sheila asked.

"Walled cities usually are," Dian replied.

Sheila decided to ignore the jibe. "How are we going to get in?"

"The same way everyone else is," Dian said in a bored tone. "There are gates into the city. We just go up to a gate, explain who we are and what we want, and then they let us in."

"Oh, great," Sheila muttered. "My name is Sheila McCarthy and I ride with the Unicorn Queen and I've come to Ansar to get some cloth for disguises so we can break into Dynasian's fortress."

Dian snorted with laughter. "Let me do the talking, all right?"

Sheila shrugged, but thought that for once it was probably a good idea.

A line had formed in front of an iron gate in the wall. Two of Dynasian's soldiers stood guard, and a shiver ran through Sheila as she recognized the menacing helmets and armor. The line moved slowly, and she began to get nervous. The soldiers were obviously questioning everyone carefully, and she hadn't even thought of a good alibi. She had always been a terrible liar. What if she slipped up and they caught her at it? What would happen if they questioned her and Dian separately and their stories didn't match?

"Listen," Dian said in a low voice, "if they question you, answer with words in your language that can't possibly translate in this time. Then I'll explain you're my cousin from across the sea who doesn't speak any of the languages of the empire. Understand?"

Sheila understood but didn't really believe it would work. Her stomach did somersaults as she waited. At last the elderly couple in front of them passed through the gate and it was Sheila and Dian's turn.

The guards asked a series of rapid-fire questions in what Sheila recognized as Miolan, the language spoken throughout the southern part of the empire. Sheila didn't understand it at all; the southern language was almost completely different from the northern tongue spoken by the riders. But Dian answered calmly, pointing to Sheila as she went through her explanations.

"Sheila?" one of the guards asked roughly. She nodded her head, and he said something that obviously was a question.

Sheila looked at Dian desperately and got the usual

bored expression. It was entirely up to her, and her mind was going blank.

The guard repeated her name, then asked another sharp question.

Frantically, Sheila searched her mind for a phrase that they couldn't translate. Of course! The name of Dr. Reit's time machine, the device that had gotten her into this mess in the first place.

"Molecular Acceleration Transport Device," she answered clearly.

The two guards gave her a puzzled look, then held a hurried conference. With a grunt the taller guard waved the girls through.

"Where did you learn to speak Miolan?" Sheila asked.

"My mother was from the south," Dian answered brusquely. "Now, just keep walking."

Sheila was fascinated by the city that lay behind the walls. The first thing that hit her was the salt tang of the sea, but all she could see was the thick web of streets crowded with shops and houses.

"Where's the water?" she asked Dian.

"I think the harbor's south." Dian pointed down one of the wider streets that was paved with stone. Like all the other streets, it took a sudden curve, so it was impossible to see to its end. Ansar looked like a puzzle designed by a madman. A street would go straight for about twenty yards, then curve, curve again, and double back on itself.

"We've got to find a shop that sells cloth," Dian said.

Sheila looked at the colorful maze of shops and stalls that surrounded them. Rows of clay jars and bowls filled one doorway, fruits and vegetables another, gleaming brass bowls and lanterns a third. The sweet scent of fresh-baked bread wafted up from the end of the street, and Sheila realized she was starving. After all, they hadn't eaten since they left camp early this morning.

"I have an idea," Sheila said. "Why don't we buy some bread for lunch, and we can ask the shopkeeper where to find the cloth."

Dian shot her a scornful look. "We can't afford to attract *anyone's* attention. Tell your stomach to be patient."

"Look," Sheila began angrily. She was tired of Dian acting like such a know-it-all. But Dian ignored her and walked briskly ahead, turning the corner of yet another narrow lane. With a sigh, Sheila followed. She felt as if she was being led into the heart of a maze.

The street that Dian had entered was even narrower than the others, and smelled of leather goods. Here the crowded stalls were filled with sandals, tanned hides, and saddles. It didn't seem like the place to find cloth, but Dian turned another corner, and suddenly they were in a lane where the leather gave way to weavers' shops and stores that sold dye and sacks filled with raw cotton.

For a moment Sheila lost sight of Dian, and then Dian emerged from a small shop. She stood waiting for Sheila to catch up.

Sheila peered into the open doorway of the shop, where wooden shelves were piled high with neatly folded fabric. They had obviously come to the right place.

"Have you ever stolen anything?" Dian asked abruptly.

"No," Sheila admitted.

"That's what I thought. Of all the people for Myno to give me—"

"I wasn't *given* to anyone," Sheila retorted. "Besides, we're not actually stealing. You have the silver, don't you?"

Dian lifted the pouch at her side. "Here's what we'll do," she said. "You'll go into the shop first and distract the shopkeeper. Ask about cloth, the weather, anything. Just keep him busy. Meanwhile, I'll get the cloth and leave the money. When you hear me cough, you'll know I'm leaving. Wait a few seconds and then follow me out."

"What if he doesn't speak our language?"

"He does," Dian answered. "I went about halfway in and heard him. You won't have any problems as long as you don't say anything stupid."

That does it, Sheila thought. *One more remark like that, and you're on your own.*

"Go ahead," Dian said, giving her a push toward the shop. "Keep him busy."

Sheila resisted the impulse to punch Dian in the nose, and instead concentrated on pretending to shop for material. It wasn't hard to fake interest. The fabrics were beautiful. She found herself drawn to a shelf of silk—rich purples, emerald greens, and a red cloth edged with golden thread. She thought of the times she had bought material for home ec class—corduroys, denim, and once some horrible satiny stuff that kept getting stuck in the sewing machine. She had never seen anything like these silks. This was the kind of stuff that princesses in fairy tales wore.

"There's something you like?" asked a smooth voice behind her.

Sheila turned to see the shopkeeper, a round middle-aged man with dark hair slicked back from his face.

"Yes," Sheila said.

The shopkeeper looked at her expectantly. Clearly, he was waiting for a more specific answer.

"I mean, I—I like them all," Sheila said truthfully.

The shopkeeper raised his eyebrows.

Oh, this is going well, Sheila thought. *We're carrying on a great conversation here.* She forced herself to think of a question: "Where are the silks from?"

"From Ansar, of course," the man said in a voice that

let her know she had just asked a dumb question. The merchant's eyes narrowed. "Do you want to buy?"

"I—I'm just looking now," Sheila said. "I want to buy a gift for my . . . my sister . . . and I've been looking all day."

"You're alone?" the shopkeeper asked in a surprisingly concerned tone.

Sheila wondered if she was making a mistake when she answered, "Yes." The shopkeeper was making her very nervous.

"Young girls shouldn't walk alone in this city," he said gruffly. "The people are uneasy . . . things have been seen."

Sheila turned her head to check on Dian. Near the back of the shop Dian was examining the cloth the way any customer might. For a supposedly accomplished thief she was certainly taking her sweet time about stealing.

Sheila brought her attention back to the shopkeeper and tried to sound interested in what he'd said last. "Why is the city uneasy?"

She fully expected to hear another story of Dynasian's soldiers harrassing the citizens and so was unprepared for his answer. "Our streets are haunted," the man said quietly.

"Haunted?" Sheila had seen a lot of strange things since entering this world, but ghosts were not among them.

The shopkeeper nodded. "An apparition of an old man. He appears and then vanishes and then reappears. Our seers say he is searching for something—or someone."

"Tell me"—Sheila could barely control her excitement—"do you know what he looks like?"

"Everyone knows. He is tall, thin, with white hair. He wears a strange white tunic and light leggings . . ."

It was Dr. Reit—Sheila was sure of it! It had been

almost a month since Sheila had seen her friend. The last time the scientist had appeared in this world had been the night she and Illyria had been held in Dynasian's prison. It was Dr. Reit's ghostly form that had made their escape possible. And while Sheila had been incredibly glad to see him, she had been dismayed to learn that he didn't know how to get her back to her own world. Worse, he didn't know if he would ever be able to find her again. Now he had been seen in Ansar. That must mean he was searching for her.

"Where was the ghost last seen?" Sheila asked, trying to sound suitably scared.

But before the shopkeeper could answer, Sheila heard a furious coughing behind her. Dian had taken the cloth and was ready to leave.

"Um—I have to go now," she said hurriedly. "Thanks for warning me about the ghost."

Quickly she made her way toward Dian and almost started laughing. The slim, athletic girl had hidden the cloth inside her dress and now looked positively fat. Without speaking the girls left the shop. Dian was walking with a weird waddle.

"Did you leave the silver?" Sheila asked. She had grown to like the shopkeeper and felt bad about taking the cloth this way.

Dian looked pale. "I forgot."

"You what?"

"You try hiding enough material to clothe eight people, and see what you remember!"

"Then give it to me now," Sheila demanded as they rounded a corner onto a street that smelled of cinnamon and spices.

"Why? What are you going to do?"

"I'm going to leave it for him, of course."

Dian's strong hand gripped Sheila's wrist. "Are you crazy?" she demanded, shaking her. "We can't afford to go back in there."

Sheila had about had it with Dian. She reached out and ripped the leather purse from Dian's side, then before the other girl could protest, she ran back toward the shop.

"You, girl, stop!" bellowed an angry voice.

Sheila looked up in alarm to see the shopkeeper running toward her.

"Thief!" he screamed. "You leave my shop and my goods leave with you!"

Oh, no, Sheila thought. This was not the way things were supposed to turn out. Quickly she tossed the pouch of coins toward the shopkeeper, then never even knowing if he stopped to pick them up, she turned and ran.

She knew that she couldn't lead him to Dian—Dian who actually had the stolen goods. Cursing the bulky dress, she ran for all she was worth.

Behind her she could hear the shopkeeper's footsteps. She just prayed it was only the shopkeeper. If he called the soldiers, she wouldn't have a chance. She tore down the narrow streets, with no idea of where she was going. Then she saw it—a large coil of hemp on the side of the street, a perfect place to hide.

Sheila crouched down behind the coil of rope and caught her breath as the shopkeeper ran past. But the man realized almost at once that she was no longer ahead of him. He stopped and turned, eyeing the row of stalls suspiciously. Sheila scrunched even lower behind the rope. It was only a matter of time now before he found her unless . . . unless she distracted him. Sheila grinned as she remembered his being frightened of the ghost. Then she reached for her backpack and pulled out her tape player. She would need a man's voice, and the stronger the better. Quickly she grabbed a Springsteen tape and put it in, pressed the "on" button, turned the volume all the way up, and sauntered out into the street.

"There you are, you little—" The shopkeeper's angry words were cut off as Springsteen's voice began to pound out the words to "Born to Run." *Very funny, Bruce,* Sheila thought as she watched the shopkeeper back away from her.

"That ghost you spoke of," Sheila said, in what she hoped was her spookiest voice. "His spirit has found me. He travels with me now. Listen . . ."

She stepped closer to the man, the music moving with her. "He says," she went on, "to tell you that I haven't stolen anything, and you are to leave me alone."

The shopkeeper's face had gone completely white, and as Springsteen's voice rose in an urgent call to "run," Sheila decided it was time to take the Boss's advice. In as dignified a manner as possible, she turned her back on the frightened man and sought the nearest gate out of Ansar.

5

❧❖❧

The Rebel Leader

Sheila never did meet up with Dian on her way out of the city. She half-expected that Dian had made it out of Ansar and would be waiting for her somewhere on the road. But as she walked toward the riders' camp, there was no sign of the other girl. In fact, there weren't many people at all once she was beyond the outskirts of the city. The road narrowed as it wound back into the hills, and Sheila began to feel completely alone. What if Dian hadn't made it? What if she had been captured? How would Sheila ever explain to Illyria?

It was late afternoon, as far she could tell, and the road still wound on. She hoped she would recognize the turn that led to the camp. She hoped she would make it back before dark.

Sheila looked up at the sound of hoofs—incredibly light hoofs. Wildwing, with Darian on his back, was racing toward her. Darian brought the white unicorn to a stop and looked down at her with an expression she couldn't figure out—happy, relieved, and a little angry all at once.

"Are you all right?" he asked.

"I'm fine," Sheila answered. "But what about Dian? We—we left Ansar separately."

"We noticed," he said dryly. "Dian's been back for a while. Nanine's already sewing disguises." He looked at Sheila's outfit and grinned. "I think the new ones are going to be an improvement over *that* thing."

"Thanks a lot," Sheila muttered, trying not to smile. Then she realized what Darian was risking. "What are you doing out on Wildwing? You know it's dangerous to ride so close to the city."

"I was looking for you," he answered gruffly. "Myno said you'd be fine, but . . . come on." He held out a hand to her. "It'll be nightfall before you get back if I let you keep walking."

To her surprise, Darian pulled her up so that she was sitting in front of him in the saddle. That meant she'd be the one riding Wildwing.

"Will he let me?" she asked Darian. Wildwing was a stallion and, as his name suggested, one of the wilder unicorns. She had seen him break into a careening gallop that even Darian had trouble controlling.

"Will you?" Darian asked the animal.

Wildwing whinnied in answer.

Darian smiled. "He says he'll give you a try."

Sheila leaned forward and stroked the unicorn's strong neck. "That's very kind of you," she told the animal. Then she gently pressed her knees into his side and the unicorn turned toward the camp.

Even with two riders on his back, Wildwing streaked effortlessly down the road. Sheila had never felt so much power in her life. With a laugh, she leaned forward and held on to the black mane, and the unicorn stretched out into a full gallop. Behind her, Darian's hands tightened around her waist, and he called out something she couldn't hear above the sound of the rushing wind.

This is freedom, Sheila thought. Not worrying about

school or parents or any of the hundreds of perfectly boring things she used to worry about—just racing the wind, and knowing that whatever happened to her in this world would be an adventure.

When Wildwing finally stopped at the entrance to the canyon, Sheila's arms were trembling from holding on so tightly. Behind her, Darian's grip on her waist loosened, and she heard him draw a deep breath.

"That was great," she said, turning to look at him.

"Yeah. Great." He gave her a curious look. "Didn't you hear me shouting at you?"

She shook her head. "I couldn't hear anything over the wind. What'd you say?"

"I told you to slow down."

"Oh, that was helpful advice," Sheila said, grinning. "Do you really think I could have slowed him if I wanted to?" She slid off Wildwing and ran her hand along the unicorn's jaw.

"I don't know," Darian said, "but it didn't seem like you were trying very hard."

"Of course not." Sheila gave the unicorn a conspirator's wink. "It was too much fun."

As Sheila and Darian walked the unicorn into the camp, Sheila saw that Dian had indeed returned, and the women were eagerly experimenting with her purchases. Most of them stood by the edge of the stream in the last light of the day, staring at their reflections as they draped and arranged the material over themselves.

Sheila stopped short at the weird scene. She had never thought she would see this hardened band of warriors making such a fuss over themselves. Even Myno was holding a piece of saffron yellow cloth to her, as if to see whether or not it complemented her red hair. It did.

Pelu ran up to them, folds of pale blue cloth draped over her arm. "Can you believe it?" she asked. "We're actually going to look respectable again. I can't wait to see Myno in that saffron."

"I can't believe this," Sheila said. "They're all acting like . . ."

"Like women?" Pelu asked with a laugh. "There's nothing that says we can't be seasoned warriors and still like pretty new clothes."

"I guess," Sheila admitted, but somehow this didn't fit her image of the riders.

Pelu held the light blue cloth up against Darian. "No, I don't think it's quite your color," she teased, and was rewarded with a scowl. She turned to Sheila, trying to keep a straight face. "You'd better go down to the water and pick out something for yourself before it's all taken."

After her part in "buying" the cloth, Sheila would have been very happy never to have to look at the stuff again. As much as she wanted to get out of the horrible tent dress, she had no desire to wear the fabric she had almost gotten captured for.

"I think I'll just change into my old tunic," Sheila said, heading back to where her tent with Kara had stood the night before. There were a few things she wanted to think about anyway—like whether or not she would have to return to Ansar to find Dr. Reit.

With a smile Sheila realized that a small, neatly lashed lean-to had replaced the tent. Sheila's sleeping roll had been carefully laid out in its shadow, and Kara sat beside it, her braid hanging over her shoulder, as she concentrated on restringing one of her bows.

"Did you have a good time in Ansar?" Kara asked without looking up.

"I wouldn't exactly call it a good time. But we got the material."

"You mean Dian got the material." Kara finished stringing her bow and tossed her long braid over her back. When she looked up at Sheila, her eyes were hard with anger. "Dian told us you went back to pay the merchant. That was honest—and foolish. And it was even more foolish of Darian to go after you on Wildwing. We cannot afford such heroism from either of you. Do you understand me?"

Sheila couldn't believe what she hearing. Kara had never snapped at her before. In fact, except for an archery lesson when Sheila had been even more uncoordinated than usual, she had never seen Kara look irritated. Among the riders Kara was known for her unshakable calm.

"Do you understand?" Kara repeated.

"I wasn't trying to be heroic," Sheila replied stiffly. "I thought if we didn't pay the man, there was more risk we'd be caught as thieves."

"There's less risk of being caught the farther you are from Ansar. You should never have gone back." Kara's face paled. "They could have gotten you, too."

Sheila had no answer for that. She knew Kara was talking about her younger sister Lianne, who had been captured by Dynasian's soldiers. Lianne was the reason Kara had joined the riders. As Illyria had sworn to free the unicorns, Kara had sworn to find and free her sister. Sheila knew Kara had been sick with disappointment when no one had been able to find a trace of Lianne in Campora. She wondered if there was any possibility that the girl was in Ansar.

Kara stood up abruptly, as if impatient with the whole conversation. "And get out of that ridiculous dress. You're lucky you didn't have to fight in that thing."

"Whew!" Sheila breathed as the archer stalked away. She changed back into her cutoffs and Darian's ragged tunic and then went to help with dinner.

The riders took turns at various chores, and this week both Sheila and Nanine were assigned to prepare the fire for the evening meal. Starting the fire usually wasn't so bad, but it was always a pain to draw enough water to boil for cooking and cleaning up afterward.

Sheila reached the fire pit and found Darian edging it with stones. "Nanine's busy sewing," he explained. "So Illyria volunteered me as her substitute. I'll go get the water if you'll start the fire."

Sheila pulled a flint and a small piece of iron from the leather drawstring pouch that hung from her waist. When she had first been asked to help with the fires, she had "cheated"—by using the matches that had been in her backpack. Now she had exactly five matches left, and she knew better than to waste them on anything less than an emergency. With a sigh, she gathered a small pyramid of twigs on the ground and then began to strike the flint and iron together. This always took patience.

She had just gotten the first sparks from the flint when she heard the unicorns' shrill warning. The animals who had been at the stream's edge were suddenly moving toward the mouth of the canyon. And within an instant every rider had responded to their call. Without thinking, Sheila drew her knife and scanned the canyon walls, looking for a sign of the enemy. Nanine, Pelu, and Myno, who were already close to the canyon's entry, had their spears drawn. The unicorns moved in behind them in restless formation. Morning Star's horn was lowered, ready to charge. The stallions, Quiet Storm and Wildwing heading them, were rearing up, their forelegs lashing out in angry challenge.

Pelu turned to the herd, her eyes flashing. "No," she told them, "we'll handle this one on our own."

After Illyria, Pelu seemed to have the most influence

over the animals, but no one could be sure of the unicorns' response. As much as they seemed to like and want to help the riders, they were creatures of the wild. Pelu looked slightly surprised when they quieted at her command. But the animals remained where they were, and it was clear that they would need little provocation to charge.

Cautiously the three riders went forward, their spears before them. Sheila watched them disappear into the mouth of the canyon. For a long moment there was silence. Then Pelu, Nanine, and Myno reappeared, and in their midst was a tall, muscular man with long red hair that streamed down past his shoulders. He wore a simple tunic, unadorned except for a gold clasp on the shoulder. He looked unimpressed by the three spears pointed at his throat.

Illyria, her sword drawn, pushed her way through the crowd of unicorns and riders. "Who are you?" she demanded.

The stranger motioned to the spears at his throat.

"Let him speak," she ordered.

The three warriors raised their spears slightly, and as they did the unicorns again prepared to fight.

"Please," he said, addressing the unicorns as much as the riders, "I come unarmed."

Illyria ignored the stranger for a moment, absorbed in the animals and whatever it was they were trying to tell her. She walked over to Quiet Storm, who danced nervously at the head of the herd. Speaking in a low voice, she managed to calm him and the others.

Then she turned to Myno. "Check him for weapons."

The stranger was searched. As he had said, he was unarmed.

"This is a warm welcome from comrades," he commented when Myno had done with him.

"Comrades?" The unicorn queen's voice was icy with contempt. "You haven't even told us who you are."

"I haven't been given much of a chance," he answered evenly. "My name is Nemor. I was a captain in Dynasian's armies. I led the Ninth Regiment." He hesitated a moment, as if seeing the past he described. "My troops won him many conquests. We took cities, villages, farms, captives . . . always captives. After a while, I became sickened by what I saw . . . and what I did. Finally I left Dynasian, but I'd spent my entire life fighting, and I grew bored without battles. I decided I would fight the tyrant himself. For the last two years I have led a band of rebels called the Sareen."

Yvere had said he would find them, and now here he was. Like the other riders, Sheila measured the man who claimed to lead the rebel forces. He was the kind of man she had come to recognize as belonging solely to this world. No matter how hard a guy from her time worked out, there was no way he could look quite like this. Nemor's tall frame was lean and muscled, and his arms bore the unmistakable scars of battle. He had the same "coiled" quality Sheila saw in Illyria and Kara, and sometimes in Darian—as if at any moment, from any position, he could explode, unleashing his power. If a man like Nemor was not an ally, he would be dangerous indeed.

Apparently, Illyria had come to the same conclusion. "I have heard of the Sareen," she told him, "but why should I believe you are their leader?"

"Lady," he answered softly, "you are not the only one with a price on your head. I come to your camp unarmed. All you need do is turn me over to the nearest soldier, and you would be rewarded with enough gold to"—he looked at the scruffy armed band that surrounded him—"to deck yourselves in jewels."

"We don't need jewels," Myno told him.

"That's good," Nemor said with a hint of a smile. "I was not counting on being turned in by my allies. I came unarmed, at substantial risk, to prove to you that I am not an enemy."

"That doesn't prove anything," said Kara.

"If you're a friend," Illyria said, "then tell me how you found us."

Nemor gestured again to the spears that were still aimed at his throat. "I promise I'll answer all your questions, but can't we at least talk in a friendlier manner?"

Sheila couldn't help smiling. The riders were not giving Nemor an easy time of it, yet he refused to be riled.

Illyria nodded and Nemor was led into the camp, where he and Illyria sat in front of her tent.

"Now," he began, "as to how I found you . . . I am skilled at tracking; it's something I've done since I was a child. And I had help from the people who know that the Sareen also seek to free the unicorns. There are over a hundred who fight with me, and many others who do not fight but aid us with food, shelter, and information."

A *hundred!* To Sheila, who was now used to the idea of fighting with a band of eight, the number was dizzying.

"With so many fighters of your own, what could you possibly want of us?" Illyria asked.

Nemor smiled, and Sheila realized how handsome he was. He had strong, broad cheekbones, and sparkling eyes that were nearly amber. His mane of red hair was streaked with gold, his skin tanned to a deep bronze. She began to understand the name "Warriors of the Sun." Nemor looked like some barbaric sun god, even in the simple brown tunic that wasn't in much better shape than her own.

"What I want," Nemor said, answering Illyria's question, "is to take Dynasian's fortress. You know he holds unicorns there. We can free them and break his hold on Ansar. There are two ways into the fortress—one is the road he has carved; the other is a footpath up the side of the mountain that few men know of." He laughed soundlessly. "Dynasian has a nasty habit of killing anyone who discovers the second route. I mean to take that route and throw open the gates to the Sareen. When I do, I want your riders and the unicorns to be the first through the gates, launching the attack." He eyed Quiet Storm with interest. "I have heard the unicorns are unmatched in battle. Even with a hundred men, I will need all the allies I can get if we're to have a chance of defeating Dynasian. We would make strong allies, Lady."

For a few moments there was only the sound of the stream running, cold and clear and having nothing to do with battles or tyrants.

"It's a bold plan," Illyria said at last.

Nemor shrugged. "I know of no subtle way to storm a fortress."

She laughed at that. "Well said. But I don't order my riders into missions. This is something that they will have to choose. Give us two days and I'll have an answer for you."

"That's too long," Nemor said. "I'll send for your answer tomorrow night."

Sheila couldn't be quite sure how it happened, but somewhere during that last exchange the power had shifted from Illyria to Nemor. It made her uneasy, and at the same time it made her admire Nemor even more. She had never seen anyone best the Unicorn Queen.

Nemor stood up with a smooth, animal grace. "I'll leave you now." With a slight inclination of his head he bowed to Illyria, and then began to walk toward the mouth of the canyon. He stopped for a moment as he passed Quiet Storm. "You *are* a beauty," he said, holding his hand out for the animal to sniff.

The unicorn tossed his head angrily, his silver horn nearly slicing open Nemor's hand. But the stranger moved with lightning reflexes and pulled his hand back before the unicorn could touch him.

"You're lucky you move quickly, Nemor. Still, if I were you, I wouldn't get so close." Illyria's soft warning held a note of mockery that took back whatever advantage Nemor had held.

He turned to her, still remarkably calm. "As you say, Lady." Then with another bow he left the camp.

6

❧ ❖ ❧

Practice

Sheila rolled over on her side, trying to find a comfortable hollow for her shoulder. She was used to sleeping on the ground, but tonight she was restless. Maybe it was because Kara hadn't yet returned to the lean-to. She, Myno, and Nanine had been cloistered in Illyria's tent ever since Nemor had left the camp. Sheila wondered if Kara was still angry with her. She hoped not; she was dying to ask her what they were going to do about Nemor's offer.

There was a soft sound Sheila couldn't identify, and then someone sat down next to her. Sheila bolted up with a start.

"Relax," Kara said with a laugh. "It's just me."

Kara had taught herself to move soundlessly, which was great until she materialized out of the night beside you. Then it was positively spooky. The archer began to unlace a sandal. "Sorry. I forgot you're not used to it."

Well, at least she doesn't sound angry, Sheila thought with relief. Tentatively, she asked, "You're not mad anymore?"

Kara's dark eyes regarded her gravely. "What I said to you had to be said, but if you'll do your best not to repeat the mistake, I think we can let the matter drop."

Sheila nodded her head in agreement.

"Besides," Kara added softly, "I was worried about you. I don't think I could stand it if the same thing happened to you that . . ." She let the sentence trail off, unable to finish it. "Now, tell me, what did you think of our new friend, Nemor?"

"He's impressive," Sheila replied honestly.

"I thought so, too," the archer admitted. "But then, I'd heard of him before. When Nemor led the Ninth Regiment, they were the most feared of all of Dynasian's troops."

"He seemed very sure of himself."

"That comes from being a fighter. And it's a safe bet he's a good one. Did you see how quickly he got his hand away from Quiet Storm? Anyone else would have been gored."

"But you don't trust him," Sheila guessed.

Kara loosened her braid and began to brush out her long, brown hair. "The point is the unicorns don't trust him. Pelu thinks he's poison."

Sheila knew that among the unicorns' powers was the unerring ability to sense danger. Illyria had not even trusted Sheila until Quiet Storm had given her his approval. The unicorn's violent reaction to Nemor was a warning that could not be ignored.

"Well, if we know he's dangerous, then what's the problem? Illyria can just say we're not going to join forces with him."

"It's not that simple," Kara answered. "Illyria doesn't trust him any more than Quiet Storm does, but she wants to get into Dynasian's fortress and free the unicorns. She thinks she can use Nemor to get us in."

"He doesn't look like the type who's easily used," Sheila said thoughtfully.

Kara gave her hair one last stroke and settled down to sleep. "That's the general opinion."

Sheila turned at the lazy tone. "You don't sound very worried."

In the moonlight she could see Kara's grin. "One enemy's like another . . . except this one's handsomer than most . . ." Her voice trailed off, and Sheila was sure she'd fallen asleep until she added, "There's only one thing about Nemor that worries me: How did he ever get so close to the camp before the unicorns sensed him?"

Sheila was up early the next morning, mostly because she was starving. With all the previous night's commotion about Nemor, no one had bothered to go hunting, and supper had consisted of flat loaves of bread and a stringy yellow plant that Pelu assured them was edible.

She found Darian cooking a porridge by the fire and giving Pelu dark looks. "And don't expect me to eat any more of whatever that was," he was saying to her. "You wouldn't dare feed anything that tasteless to the unicorns, and you know it."

"No one forced you to eat it," Pelu told him, grinning. She was wearing a tunic sewn from the new material. Its sky-blue weave brought out the blue of her eyes and that, combined with her delicate build, somehow made her look young and very innocent. No one would ever take her for a warrior.

"Want breakfast?" Darian asked Sheila. "I guarantee it's an improvement over last night."

Sheila accepted a bowl of the porridge as Pelu neatly stepped behind Darian, grabbed his wrist, and applied pressure.

"Do you apologize for all your nasty comments about dinner?" the healer asked sweetly.

Darian twisted against her grasp, found himself unable to break free, and swore under his breath.

Pelu waited patiently until he apologized.

"You'd better learn to choose your opponents more carefully," Illyria said with a laugh as she came upon Darian rubbing his wrist and glaring at Pelu. She sat down beside Sheila, helped herself to her brother's cooking, and winked at her youngest rider. "Well, at least he can cook."

Myno strode over to the group, a vision in saffron. Nanine had fashioned a longish tunic for her that hung in soft, graceful folds. But even Nanine's skill couldn't diminish Myno's powerful presence. Sheila was sure that if you dressed Myno in a twentieth-century lace wedding gown, she would still look as if she were about to charge into battle. "I want everyone over here now!" she barked.

Nanine and Dian came up from the stream, and Kara materialized from wherever she had been. Morning Star, her curiosity aroused, poked her head into the circle. "Not you," Sheila said fondly, and pushed her away.

Meanwhile Myno had begun. The day's mission, she announced, was for the band to split up, go into Ansar and the surrounding villages on foot, and gather as much information as they could about the Sareen, Nemor, and Dynasian's fortress. "Nanine and Pelu, you'll go into Ansar; Darian, the village just north of the city; Kara, Illyria, and I will cover the settlements in the hills. Dian and Sheila will remain in camp."

"Why?" both girls cried at once.

"Because," Illyria answered, "after yesterday, I'm not going to risk either one of you being recognized. And since Nemor found us, there's the possibility that someone else will. I don't want to leave the unicorns unguarded."

Sheila couldn't believe it. Two days in a row, stuck with Dian!

"Don't worry," Myno said, "I'll leave you plenty to keep you busy."

Within an hour the others had taken off and Sheila and Dian were left staring at a lengthy list of things to do. First they had to clean up after breakfast, then each girl was to do the sewing on the tunic that Nanine had cut out for her; there were saddle girths to be mended, and swords to be polished. And that was just the morning. The afternoon, Myno had specified, was to be spent in sword practice.

Sheila moaned as she envisioned the day ahead. "You know what this is, don't you?" she asked her fellow laborer. "This is Myno finally getting us back for that night when we were arguing about the saddles."

Dian shrugged. "It doesn't matter what it's for. Let's just get it over with."

They spent a good deal of time cleaning up after breakfast. Darian had managed to burn the porridge to the bottom of the pot, and it took forever to scrub it off in the cold stream.

As she had the day before, Dian barely spoke a word to Sheila, and as far as Sheila was concerned, that was just fine. But both girls had a pleasant surprise when they went to Nanine's tent and found the tunics she had cut for them. Nanine had worked hard to make sure that no two were the same, so that the riders wouldn't look like a troop.

Dian loved the color green and Nanine had left her a long, light green tunic, slit high at the sides. Even Sheila had to admit that Dian looked lovely when she slipped it on.

"I'll have to cut it," Dian said wistfully as she stared at her reflection in the water. "I mean once we really start riding again."

Sheila wouldn't have that problem. The tunic Nanine had cut for her was short and woven from a lavender fabric so soft it reminded her of flannel. Sheila had never really liked lavender before, but this shade seemed just right with her auburn hair, tanned skin, and hazel eyes. For the first time in weeks she felt pretty, and she couldn't help wondering what Darian would think when he saw her.

The afternoon was half gone by the time Sheila and Dian had worked their way down Myno's list to "sword practice." This was the part of the day Sheila had been dreading. The truth was, she liked sword lessons when they were with Illyria or even Myno. Illyria had given her Darian's old sword, and gradually Sheila had relaxed enough to realize that using the sword well had more to do with skill and speed than with strength. But she had never worked with Dian before. All she knew was that everyone in the camp agreed that when it came to weapons, Dian was a natural.

"We'll work down by the stream," Dian decided. "The ground's level there."

Grimly, Sheila tightened her hold on her sword and followed Dian. Both girls had remained in their old tunics for this, knowing they would wind up sweaty and probably dirty as well.

"Now," Dian said with a superior tone, "why don't we start with basic drills."

Sheila had done hours of basic drills with both Illyria and Myno, but she wasn't about to tell this to Dian.

"Front thrust, retreat, block, and upper cut," Dian ordered.

Sheila did as she was told, following Dian's motions. In spite of herself, she had to admit that Dian was really good. Like Illyria and Darian, her cuts were smooth and sure. The sword never wobbled or tilted at odd angles. And though they were practicing four separate moves, Dian had a way of blending them into a seamless whole.

They practiced basics until Sheila thought her arm was going to fall off.

"Good," Dian said at last. "Let's see you spar."

"Now?" Sheila panted. "Give me a minute to catch my breath."

"I can just see it," Dian scoffed. "In the middle of a battle you'll look up at Dynasian's soldiers and say, 'Could I have a minute to catch my breath, please?' "

"Forget I even asked," Sheila said angrily. "I'm ready whenever you are."

Usually when they sparred, the warriors would warm up with a set of prearranged moves, with one person attacking and the other defending. Dian dispensed with that as she announced, "No rules. Open fight."

"Fine," Sheila said, though the thought of going into an open match against Dian rattled her. She knew Dian was going to try something; it was just a question of what.

Dian took her by surprise by fighting fairly. The problem was, she was about five times better than Sheila and, unlike Illyria and Myno, had no qualms about using her full strength against a less-skilled opponent. Dian's sword whirled and met Sheila's with a ringing blow. Then before Sheila could counter the move, Dian was attacking again, relentless and tireless.

After a while Sheila lost count of the number of times she either had the sword knocked out of her hand or found herself knocked off her feet. When Dian finally managed to accomplish both with one move, Sheila decided she had had enough. Her teeth ached from being jarred so hard, and her left arm was shaking so badly she could barely close her hand around the sword's hilt. The worst part was that she hadn't scored a single hit on Dian. Not one.

She blinked back hot tears as Dian came to stand in front of her. "Get up," the other girl ordered, "you're not done."

"Yeah, but you are," said an angry voice behind them. "Maybe the reason she's having such a hard time is because her teacher isn't very good." Darian planted himself between Sheila and Dian, his sword drawn. "I don't think," he said to Dian, "that you'd like me to give *you* the kind of lesson you just gave her."

"You're interfering," Dian said angrily.

Sheila got to her feet, feeling a mixture of relief and embarrassment. The last thing she wanted was Dian thinking she needed Darian to protect her. "I'm fine," she announced. "And . . . and I'll continue, if you want."

"Why?" Darian asked. "So you can get even more worn out and discouraged?"

"Darian, please!" Sheila couldn't believe he was being so dense about this.

"I need practice, too," he announced with a cocky grin. "So I'll fight either one of you."

"You're acting like a bully, and you're pampering her!" Dian said.

"If you want to fight me, draw your sword," Darian replied, his own sword balanced lightly in front of him. "I'm waiting, O great teacher."

"Well, then, you'll wait!" Dian spat. Without another word, she grabbed her sword and stalked off toward her tent.

"I wish you hadn't done that," Sheila said when they were alone.

Darian now stood staring into the stream, as if the scene with Dian had never happened. "Catch your breath," he said, without looking at Sheila. "Then pick up your sword and we'll see that you learn something."

"Darian, I'm serious. If Dian thinks you're protecting me . . ."

"What Dian thinks doesn't matter." He turned to face her, and for once there was no spark of humor in Darian's dark eyes. "What matters is that you learn to fight without losing the confidence you've built so far. Beating you into the ground isn't the way to do it. Now, pick up that sword and stop wasting time."

Sighing, Sheila picked up the sword again. With a sense of surprise she realized that the blade felt completely natural in her hand, as if she had used one all her life. Illyria had once promised that eventually the sword would feel like an extension of her arm—and now it was happening.

Still, she was extremely relieved when Darian announced that they would start with the prearranged combinations. "I'll attack, you defend," he said.

He began slowly, so that Sheila could follow the movement of his sword and meet it with her own. Darian's sword carved precise lines through the air, and though Sheila could rarely anticipate where the next move would come from, the blade was so perfectly controlled that she felt safe. Darian could stop the sword a hairsbreadth from her skin. And though he could have easily disarmed her or knocked her off her feet, as Dian had, he never took advantage of his strength.

Gradually, as he saw that Sheila was calmer than she had been with Dian, Darian picked up speed. Sheila parried his blows as quickly as she could, whirling to meet the sword that darted at her from above, below, and all sides.

"Easy," Darian said, his voice reassuring. "Don't let me make you rush your own moves. Fight *your* fight, not mine."

Sheila took a deep breath and concentrated on controlling her pace. She had no sooner gotten a grip on that than Darian called a break to explain that she was giving him too many openings. Then he let her work the attack and, as he defended himself, showed her how to correct the mistakes she had been making.

Bit by bit they advanced to more complicated patterns. Occasionally Darian would throw in an unexpected strike or show her a different way to use the techniques she was already familiar with. Like Illyria, he was demanding without being intimidating. He never let her relax enough to be caught off guard and yet, Sheila realized with a sense of surprise, she was actually having fun.

When Darian called for a rest sometime later, Sheila was breathing hard, soaked with sweat, and even more sore than she had been with Dian. But her eyes were shining and she was laughing.

"Better?" Darian asked.

"Much better."

"If you keep practicing, you're going to be a terror," he predicted.

Sheila put her sword back in its sheath. "You're a good teacher."

"That's because I was lucky enough to have a good one."

"Illyria?"

"Not exactly," he said quietly. "But we had the same teacher. Our father."

Sheila didn't know what to say. Neither Darian nor Illyria talked much about their home. She had a feeling that everything—and everyone—had been destroyed by Dynasian's troops. Now, with Darian so quiet, she didn't dare ask.

Finally Darian broke the awkward silence. "You

know," he said, the mischief back in his eyes, "one of the most important things my father taught me is that you've got to cool down properly after practice."

His glance slid from Sheila to the stream.

Sheila looked at the water and then back at Darian.

"Oh, no you don't," she said, understanding him all too well. She turned to run, but didn't get very far. She was exhausted and Darian was faster anyway.

"You won't need this now." Darian removed her sword from her belt as he caught her. Laughing, he picked her up and carried her to the stream.

"No!" she shrieked. "I'm too tired to swim. I'll drown. Darian, put me down now!"

"As you wish," he said with mock gallantry, and threw her into the stream.

Sheila felt the deliciously cool water close over her, and for a moment stayed beneath the surface, hoping to give Darian a scare. When she could no longer hold her breath, she sat up, sputtering, and tried to look angry.

Darian stood on the bank watching her. "I don't think you drowned," he observed.

"No thanks to you." Sheila stood up, intent on vengeance, and sat down again with a splash as the weight of her soaked tunic combined with the current to bring her down.

Darian gave up all pretense of control and doubled over laughing.

"I don't care how good you are with a sword," Sheila said, hoping she sounded angrier than she actually was. "I'll get you for this."

"Yeah? What are you going to do? Hide my sandals?"

With a very undignified screech Sheila rose and lunged toward the shore, determined to at least soak him. But Darian beat her to it, arcing into the stream with a graceful dive.

"Show-off," Sheila muttered.

A moment later he surfaced beside her. Sheila sent a jet of water into his face and swam for the opposite bank.

It was no use. Darian pulled even with her, swimming with strong, smooth strokes. "Admit it," he told her in a smug tone. "You really wanted to go swimming with me."

Sheila just rolled her eyes. She was too tired to give him the satisfaction of an argument. But they swam together until it was nearly time for dinner, and secretly she couldn't help wondering if he was right.

7

✠

Visitors

One by one the women returned to the camp. That evening they gathered around the fire to report on what they had found.

"Before any of you tell me about Nemor," Illyria began, "Kara has some news."

The archer's face was drawn as she spoke. "I spoke to a woman today who recognized my description of Lianne. She said that she had seen a chain of captives being led to Dynasian's fortress, and one of them looked like my sister."

"That's great!" Sheila said.

Kara shook her head. The others were silent.

"It's not great?" Sheila asked.

"We all know how Dynasian treats his captives," Myno said sharply. The tyrant was feared throughout the empire for his cruelty, and as an escaped slave herself, there were few who knew it better than Myno.

Illyria looked at Kara with both sympathy and a resolve to face the truth. "If we do take the fortress and find Lianne—"

"I'm not sure I want to see what we find," Kara finished, and strode from the fire.

Pelu started after her, but Illyria stopped the healer. "Let her go. Kara will be all right, but she needs time by herself. And I need to know what all of you found out about Nemor."

It seemed everything he had told them was true. He had been one of Dynasian's ablest and most trusted captains when he suddenly resigned. No one knew what explanation he gave the tyrant, but it must have been a good one, for few men left Dynasian's service alive. Nemor disappeared from sight for a while, then, approximately a year later, he showed up in one of the villages outside Ansar and began to build the rebel group the Sareen. Since then he had mounted a series of daring raids on Dynasian's troops. To Sheila, he sounded like some kind of Robin Hood, stealing from the tyrant's caravans and soldiers and giving to the poor. The people considered him a hero—and their only real hope for overthrowing Dynasian.

"Well," said Illyria when all of the riders had spoken. "It seems Nemor is beloved by the people. I, too, heard the same things wherever I asked. By all accounts, he's the perfect ally. Why, then, did Quiet Storm nearly rip him open?"

She stared into the fire, as if looking for her answer there. When she had disguised herself that morning, she had let Nanine paint lines and age spots on her face. She had assumed the hunched-over walk of an old woman, and she had taken her hair down. Now she had straightened and scrubbed off the makeup, but her hair still hung loose in waist-length silver waves. In the flickering firelight, Sheila saw a strange expression cross the Unicorn Queen's face. It was as if, just for a moment, Illyria wished she were doing anything in the world besides plotting battles and strategies. Sheila wondered if she was thinking of Laric.

"I think," Illyria said at last, "that we must work with Nemor."

"What?" Pelu was outraged. "How can you ignore the unicorns' warning?"

"I'm not ignoring anything. But if there is a way into that fortress, Nemor will know it, and I mean to get it from him. Whatever it is he's up to, I want him to play out his hand."

"Even though this game may involve considerable danger," Nanine said, as if completing the thought.

Illyria stood, a sign that the council was over. "I meant what I told Nemor. I will not order any of you into this. Each of you must choose whether or not you will risk this partnership."

"Do you really think any of us would refuse?" Myno asked with an impatient grunt.

The Unicorn Queen smiled at her band. "I mean to get more information from Nemor himself before I commit any of us to battle. But if Nemor sends for my answer, I will tell him that we will join forces." She turned to Myno with one last instruction: "Make sure you double the watch tonight."

By the time dinner was over Sheila was nearly asleep on her feet. The sword lessons with Dian and Darian had worn her out completely. She crawled into her bedroll and was asleep as soon as her head touched the ground. So it was with a sense of bewilderment that she found herself wide awake in the middle of the night.

She sat up, trying to figure out what had awakened her. The sky was still black, and beside her, Kara's bedroll was empty. The archer was on watch. The camp was quiet. There were only the sounds of the stream and the soft whickering of the unicorns.

Without quite knowing why, Sheila pulled her blanket around her shoulders cloak-style and got up. She waited a few minutes until her eyes had adjusted to the darkness

and then cautiously began to move through the camp—
cautiously because she didn't want anyone on watch mis-
taking her for an enemy.

She walked toward the back of the canyon, away from
the sleeping warriors. It wasn't a good night for walking.
A steady, dry wind blew clouds across the waxing moon,
so that she was able to see where she was going for about
a minute, only to be plunged into darkness the next.

The clouds slid across the moon again and she stopped
where she was, waiting for the light to return. And when
it did, there in the moonlight was the ghostly figure of a
tall, thin man with wild white hair.

"Dr. Reit!" Sheila cried. The scientist had been looking for her, after all. And now he'd found her. Did that
mean he had also found a way to take her back to her
own world?

"Shhhh!" he said, obviously delighted to see her. "You
don't want to wake your friends, do you?"

"I'm so glad you're here!" Sheila lowered her voice
just a fraction. If she could have hugged his shimmering
form, she would have.

"Yes, well, I've been looking for you," he explained.
"You are all right, aren't you?"

"Yes, but—" Suddenly Sheila was hit with a wave of
homesickness so sharp it nearly undid her. At that moment she would have given anything to see her family.
"Have—have you come to take me home?"

"Well, that's what I wanted to talk to you about," the
scientist answered in his usual distracted manner. "Actually, it's pure luck that I found you. You might say I
bounced right across your path."

Sheila couldn't exactly make sense of this, but that
wasn't unusual with Dr. Reit. So she asked the same question she had asked him dozens of times: "What are you
talking about?"

The scientist thrust his hands into the pockets of his lab coat with a sigh. "The problem with traveling between worlds, my dear, is crossing the molecular time warp. You just happened to fall into my time machine and wind up in this time. But for me to travel into this world and no other, I need a very specific form of acceleration—"

Sheila tried to picture the high-tech rocket Dr. Reit had probably constructed just for this purpose.

"I used a springboard," the scientist explained.

"You mean, like the kind you use in gymnastics?" Sheila asked in disbelief.

"Well, more or less. And it did get me here and will most probably get me back. However, I don't think it will do anything for your problem." Dr. Reit saw Sheila's crestfallen expression, and his form wavered with what might have been doubt. The moonlight shone straight through him. "Now, there's no reason to get downhearted," he said quickly. "You see, I'm working on a reverse mechanism that I think will get you back."

"You *think?*" Sheila echoed.

"Well, you know these things are never certain until they've been tested and retested. If I was doing this properly, I'd try it on mice first, then rats and guinea pigs, maybe rabbits . . ."

Sheila summoned all her patience. "Dr. Reit, have you found a way to get me home or not?"

"Well, that's what I've been trying to tell you, dear girl. I think I've found a way to reverse the molecular acceleration, but it requires a great deal more acceleration than I've been using up to now, and—"

"And I'm still stuck here," Sheila finished.

"Well, yes," the scientist admitted softly. "But only for a while. I promise you."

Sheila sank down against a tree. "What about my parents?" she asked in a small voice.

"They're fine, I'm sure."

Sheila wasn't sure this was good news. Of course, she didn't want anything bad to happen to her parents, but somehow she didn't like the idea of them being "fine" when she was missing.

"Oh, didn't I explain?" Distress filled his voice, and Dr. Reit's pale image wavered again and nearly vanished. "You're in a parallel universe, but the passage of time is not at all parallel. Time here has nothing to do with time back home. Though you've been here over a month now, at home it's still the same afternoon that you left. No one knows you're missing except me."

"Wonderful," Sheila said flatly. "I may get killed in some crazy battle, and no one will even know I'm gone."

"You're still trying to fight the tyrant, then?"

Sheila nodded and filled him in on all that had gone on.

"Fascinating," said Dr. Reit when she had finished. "Simply fascinating."

Sheila was about to tell him it wasn't nearly as fascinating as it was dangerous when the ghostly form before her flickered for a moment and then vanished as quickly as it had come.

Sheila let her head sink down on her knees. It had been nearly a month since Dr. Reit's last visit. Who knew when—or if—she would ever see him again. And even if she did, what was the use? He'd probably just vanish again.

"So that's the sorcerer," said a quiet voice.

Sheila jerked her head up with a start. Darian was standing beside her. He must have heard most of their conversation.

"I wish you'd stop sneaking up on me," she snapped, angry that he had spied on her. "You could have made a little noise, you know."

"I'm sorry," said the boy, sitting down next to her.

"But I was on watch. I heard voices. . . . You want to go home, don't you?"

Sheila didn't answer. She was afraid that if she started talking about home, she would start crying.

"Are you so unhappy here?" he asked gently.

"I miss my family and my friends. Even my bedroom, sometimes."

Darian's hand reached out for hers. "I don't think I'd like it if I found myself in another world. I can't even imagine yours."

"You might like it," Sheila said, trying to picture him behind the wheel of a car. Darian's hand felt so good around hers—warm and strong and comforting. "And it's not that I hate this world," she went on, suddenly wanting him to understand. "It's funny. I used to daydream about living a life filled with heroic adventures. I guess that's why I always read a lot of science fiction and fantasy."

Darian looked at her blankly, and she realized he had no idea of what she was talking about. To him this world wasn't something out of a heroic daydream. It was simply his life.

"What I mean is," she tried again, "in a lot of ways, coming here—and meeting all of you—has been the best thing that ever happened to me. But—"

She never had a chance to finish, for at that moment there was a shrill, angry whinny. In the moonlight Sheila saw Quiet Storm rear up, his powerful forelegs lashing out in a furious attack.

Darian was up and running before Sheila even realized that a man was trying to approach the unicorn, a man carrying a halter.

Without thinking, Sheila took off after Darian. "Wake up!" she cried as she raced through the camp. "Someone's after Quiet Storm!"

Near the mouth of the canyon Darian took off in a flying leap, tackling the stranger. Both of them came down hard. There was a long scuffle and Sheila couldn't tell one from the other. Then, with a grunt, Darian pulled himself up on top of the stranger, his fist raised. Above them Quiet Storm's hoofs cut through the air. With a shout the stranger twisted violently, rolling Darian beneath him. Just as Sheila reached them the stranger's arm arced up, a knife gleaming in his hand.

"No!" Sheila didn't have time to draw her own knife. She just threw herself forward, grabbing the stranger's wrist and jerking it back.

There was a blur of motion beside her and then Illyria was there, her knife at the man's throat. "Drop your weapon," she commanded, "and then get up, very slowly."

With a muttered curse, the stranger did as he was told.

"Let him go, Sheila," Illyria said.

Sheila stared at her own hand in surprise. Even though the stranger had dropped the knife, her fingers were still stiff around his wrist. With a shudder, she released him.

Myno stepped forward, grabbed the stranger's hands, and bound them tightly behind his back with a leather thong.

"Darian?" Illyria turned to her brother with concern.

Darian was on his feet, breathing hard, his head turned away from them. Sheila could see that he was cradling his right arm.

"Darian, let me see." Pelu tried to touch his arm, but he jerked away angrily, and Sheila saw the pain in his eyes. "Let me see," Pelu repeated gently.

"Do as she tells you," Illyria said, her words both a plea and a command.

With a sigh of defeat, Darian let Pelu take his arm.

She began to straighten it and then stopped. "It's broken."

Darian shrugged, as if to say, "I knew that."

"Can you set it?" Illyria asked.

Pelu's smile was grim. "I'll have to knock him out first."

"I can take the pain," Darian said gruffly.

"Not this much, you can't," Pelu told him. "Come. I'm going to brew a potion for you, and then you're going to sleep *very deeply*."

"Go with her." Illyria brushed a shock of dark hair from her brother's face. It was the tenderest gesture Sheila had ever seen between them. "I want you well soon."

Darian gave his sister a sly look. "All right, but first" —he turned to the stranger all but forgotten in the concern over his arm—"I want to hear what this snake has to say."

Illyria scowled for a moment at her brother, but when it was clear that he wouldn't give in, she turned to the stranger. Her voice was deadly calm as she asked, "Who are you?"

The man didn't reply but stared sullenly at the ground.

Behind him Kara grasped his long hair and jerked his head back. "You were asked a question," she hissed. "Now, answer before I put *my* knife in your throat."

Nanine's haughty voice cut through the night. "Does it matter who he is when we know who sent him?" She carried a makeshift torch that she now held close to the stranger's face. "Look at the necklace he wears."

A gold chain circled the man's neck and a pendant hung from it. Made of hammered gold, it looked like some sort of sun but with sharp geometric angles.

"Of course," Illyria said, with a sharp intake of breath. "He wears the same symbol Nemor wore on his tunic. He's Nemor's man. I, too, should have seen that."

"There's something else about that symbol," Nanine

said, an unusual note of worry in her voice. "I could swear I've seen it before, only I can't remember where."

Illyria reached for the pendant and dropped it as soon as she touched it, almost as if she had been burned.

"Moon above," Nanine swore softly, "I know what that is, only"—she turned to the stranger, her voice acidic—"you've changed it, haven't you?"

The man remained silent, ignoring her.

Illyria's eyes widened in recognition, but she didn't respond to Nanine. Instead she turned to the stranger. "I suppose you are the one Nemor sent for my answer."

The man nodded his head.

"Why, then," Illyria continued, "did you bring a halter?"

Obstinately the intruder continued to stare at the ground. But for the first time he spoke. "Nemor sent me to find out if you will join him to take the fortress. If you agree, you must meet him at midday tomorrow in the village of Odelia." He fell silent again.

"I think that's as much as we'll get from him," Myno decreed impatiently. "Send him back to his master."

"What?" an outraged Darian protested. "He came into our camp armed, tried to take Quiet Storm—"

"Not now!" Illyria cut him off fiercely. She sent a questioning gaze to Nanine, who nodded her assent. "Very well, then," the Unicorn Queen agreed. "Return to Nemor and give him two messages from me. The first is that I will meet him in Odelia. The second is that if he ever crosses me again, he will not live to see the next dawn."

Myno grabbed the collar of the man's cloak and roughly began to pull him out of the canyon.

"My knife," the man protested. "You don't expect me to travel these roads unarmed?"

"That's a risk you'll have to take," Myno replied.

With Myno's spear against his ribs, the stranger left the camp.

"Let me see the knife," Nanine said as soon as he was out of sight.

Kara handed her the small bronze blade. "There it is again," Nanine said. Her finger traced the strange circular pattern engraved into the widest part of the blade. "He didn't need the knife; he just didn't want us to see this."

Sheila and Darian exchanged puzzled looks, and Dian spoke for them both, "It's more than Nemor's symbol, isn't it?"

"It's called a *krino*," Nanine answered. "The one that he and Nemor wear is slightly different from the original symbol, but it's essentially the same thing."

"As what?" Darian asked, clearly reaching the limits of his patience. "What's it a symbol of?"

"Evil," Illyria answered. "The *krino* is a very old, very powerful sign of dark magic. When we were in Campora, Mardock wore a ring that was similar. It's a protection, a calling on the Dark Gods. It explains why our visitor got past the watch and why Quiet Storm didn't do him any harm. The man is a mage."

Darian turned on his sister, his eyes blazing. "And knowing that, you released him?"

"Oh, Darian." Illyria's voice held none of the anger Sheila expected. "If he is even half as powerful as Nanine suspects, do you really think I could have kept him?" she chided. "However, it is entirely within my power to see that you have your arm attended to. Now, go with Pelu, and no more arguments!"

8

❧❖❧

A Change of Plan

Odelia was one of the small hill towns on the outskirts of Ansar. It was far enough from the city for the riders to travel by unicorn, and Illyria had announced that with the exception of Darian, who was still nursing his broken arm, all of the riders would accompany her to Nemor's camp.

Her sword fastened to her waist and her backpack snugly on her back, Sheila readied Morning Star for the ride. She ran a brush along the unicorn's silky white coat. All of the unicorns were beautiful, but to Sheila Morning Star was the most beautiful of all. The mare nudged her with her head, as if impatient to leave. It had been two days since they had ridden together, and both of them had missed the other's companionship.

"Be patient a little longer," Sheila told the unicorn as she finished brushing out the thick, dark mane. "We'll be riding in just a few moments. I promise you."

"I'm afraid there's been a change of plan," Illyria said, walking up to them. She was holding a handful of greens which she offered to Morning Star. With a delicate shake of her head, the mare declined the offer.

Sheila looked at the Unicorn Queen. Illyria was dressed

to ride, as were Nanine and Myno, who stood behind her. Things didn't *look* as if they had changed.

"I need to ask a favor of you, Sheila," Illyria began. "Will you let me ride Morning Star today?"

"You mean you ride Morning Star and I ride Quiet Storm?" Sheila asked. Riding Quiet Storm was probably a lot like riding Wildwing, except Quiet Storm was even bigger and probably more dangerous.

Illyria's blue eyes were troubled when she answered. "No. No one is going to ride Quiet Storm today. I went to saddle him and he reared up, panicked. He won't let me near him." She ran her hand down Morning Star's back. "I've never seen him like this before."

"It's no mystery," said Nanine, anger close to the surface. "It was the mage—he put Quiet Storm under a spell."

Illyria sighed. "I don't know how to lift the spell, and that's something I can't even attend to now. I need your help, Sheila. I must meet with Nemor this afternoon. Morning Star is the gentlest of the unicorns. I fear I would spend half a day convincing any of the others to accept me. Will you let me borrow her? Besides," she added with a smile, "I need you to stay with Darian and Quiet Storm. Whom else would I trust with my two dearest loves?"

Sheila was disappointed, but she knew she couldn't refuse. Resigning herself to the new plan, she ran her hand through Morning Star's mane. "You'll take Illyria where she wants to go, won't you?"

Morning Star gazed at her through long white lashes, as if to be sure she meant it.

"Please," Sheila urged the mare. "And you must protect her as you would me."

The unicorn gave her a slightly reproachful look, then turned toward Illyria. She lowered her black horn, and for a moment Sheila feared that the mare was preparing to charge.

Again, Illyria held out the greens. "Come, Morning Star," she said, her voice confident and gentle. "It's only till Quiet Storm is well again."

Sheila was relieved to see that, after a moment's hesitation, the unicorn munched down her gift and allowed Illyria to mount her.

Within minutes Illyria had summoned the other riders, and they had departed for Odelia. Sheila was left with Quiet Storm, Darian, and the wild unicorns. Despite Illyria's comforting words, she was sure she had been the one left behind because she was the least-experienced warrior. And having been left in the camp the day before, she was restless. The relentless rhythm of breaking camp every day and riding for miles must have gotten into her blood. Two days in one place and she longed to be riding again.

Feeling extremely grumpy, she surveyed the camp. Most of the herd stood by the edge of the stream, drinking quietly. But at the far end of the canyon, Quiet Storm stood alone. She saw immediately why the others wouldn't go near him. The stallion's eyes were wild and his sides were heaving. As if fighting an invisible enemy, he was caught in a furious pattern—rearing up, coming down and lowering his head for a charge, and then bucking as if a demon rode him. *Oh, you poor thing,* Sheila thought, *you're trying to break the spell on your own. If we don't get you cured, you'll probably die of exhaustion.*

She turned back to the camp. Darian sat by Illyria's tent, his back against a tree, his right arm splinted and in a sling. Pelu had assured her that he was no longer in pain. He might still be groggy from the sleeping potion, she explained, but if he didn't attempt anything too heroic, he would be fine. Sheila was supposed to make sure that he rested.

Reluctantly Sheila approached her charge. She had a

feeling that telling Darian to rest would be about as effective as telling Wildwing to slow down.

"Hi," she said. "Are you feeling better?"

Darian didn't look at her, but stared at the ground. "I'm fine," he answered in a flat voice. "Quiet Storm's going crazy, and I'm just sitting here. It feels great to be absolutely useless."

"You're not—" She stopped midsentence as he looked up, his eyes nearly black with anger.

"Tell me what it is I'm good for," he challenged. "I can't fight, can't ride. I can barely stand without feeling the ground spin."

"That's just the sleeping potion. Pelu said it would wear off."

"Pelu said it would wear off," he mimicked in mincing tones.

Sheila decided he had had enough sympathy. "I'm not exactly happy about staying here, either," she told him heatedly, "especially with *you* for company. I've seen six-year-olds who handled broken arms better. You get hurt and think it's an excuse to turn into a whining, sniveling, self-pitying—"

"All right, all right." There was the faintest trace of a smile on his mouth as he held up his good arm in a gesture of surrender. "I'm sorry . . . especially because I owe you my thanks."

"For what?"

"For saving my life last night. If you hadn't caught the intruder's knife hand and held it"—he gave her a dazzling grin—"I wouldn't be sitting here giving you such a rough time."

"Don't make me regret my heroism," Sheila muttered.

Unrepentant, Darian held out his good hand. "Friends again?"

Sheila looked at him in exasperation. She had never met anyone so moody. One minute he was ready to snap her head off, the next he was charming her.

"Friends," she agreed with mock reluctance.

Darian leaned back against the tree and regarded her with lazy curiosity. "So, since I'm your patient for the day, how do you intend to amuse me?"

"Amuse you?" she sputtered, getting to her feet. "You can amuse yourself, you obnoxious—"

"Oh, Sheila, don't get mad," he broke in. "I only meant maybe you had something in your backpack."

More than any of the others, Darian had been intrigued by the contents of Sheila's backpack. Everything from the twentieth century seemed to fascinate him. With the exception of his sword, the Mickey Mouse watch Sheila had given him had become his most valued possession.

"I think you've already seen it all," Sheila answered. She was still wearing the pack; after Illyria had told her she had to stay, she hadn't bothered to take it off. Now she zipped it open and peered inside. "Maybe listening to music will improve your mood." She took out the tape player and flipped it on.

Darian looked a little unnerved at the sound of Springsteen's voice booming out at him, but watched the tape player with fascination. Sheila had already tried to explain to him how it worked, but she got stuck when it came to how the voice actually got onto the tape. She wasn't too clear about that herself.

"Do you have anything else?" Darian asked hopefully.

Sheila rummaged in the bottom of the pack. No sense wasting the matches, flashlight, or Band-Aids to impress Darian. He had already seen the notebook and pen and her mirror. She smiled as her hands closed on a pack of bubble gum.

"I've got it," she declared triumphantly, holding out a stick of gum.

Darian examined the flat, paper-wrapped object. "What does it do?"

"You chew it. But don't swallow it."

He raised an eyebrow, then dutifully started to put it in his mouth.

"Take the paper off first," Sheila suggested, trying to keep a straight face. Just to make sure he got the idea, she unwrapped a piece for herself.

Darian did as he was told and began chewing. He chewed in silence for several minutes. "It tastes good," he announced at last, "but not like food."

"It's not food," Sheila assured him.

"Then why am I chewing it?" A look of betrayal crossed his face. "This is like Pelu's herbs, a medicine. You thought you could trick me!"

Sheila giggled helplessly. "It's not food and it's not medicine. It won't do you any good at all." He looked at her menacingly. "And it won't hurt you, either," she added quickly. "I promise. Gum is just something we chew because it tastes good. And with bubble gum, which is what this is, you can blow bubbles."

Darian looked mystified as she blew a perfect pink bubble and then popped it back into her mouth. He chewed harder as she blew another.

"You can't do it by chewing," Sheila said. "Here, I'll show you how." She figured a lesson in blowing bubbles might not exactly equal one in swordplay, but at least it would help pass the time and keep Darian out of trouble.

Half an hour later Sheila and Darian were laughing so hard they could barely sit up straight. Darian had tried valiantly to blow bubbles and had succeeded only in making terrible faces. Sheila had completely given up on trying to explain; blowing bubbles was more complicated than she had realized. Secretly she was amused to have discovered one thing Darian wasn't good at.

"Let me try one more time," he gasped as a last fit of laughter passed. With tremendous concentration he chewed some more—and blew the tiniest bubble Sheila had ever seen.

"You did it!" she shouted.

"Did what, dear girl?" asked a perplexed voice.

Darian's mouth dropped open and the gum, bubble and all, fell out.

"Dr. Reit?" Sheila couldn't believe what she was seeing. The apparition of the elderly scientist got weirder every time she saw him. "What are you doing on a skateboard? And wearing hightops?"

"Do you like them?" he asked, looking quite pleased with himself. "I was told by a reliable source that one must have hightops to skateboard properly."

Sheila just shook her head in amazement.

Darian nudged her. "Oh, Dr. Reit, this is Darian, Illyria's brother. He's been wanting to meet you."

"Sheila has told us that you are a powerful sorcerer," Darian said.

Dr. Reit nodded absently in the boy's direction. "Yes, well, I wouldn't phrase it that way myself, but the general idea is velocity."

"Velocity?" Sheila asked.

"That's why I'm here on the skateboard," Dr. Reit said, as if that explained everything. For the first time he noticed their blank expressions. "You see, I've discovered that the key to traveling through time is velocity—speed. This skateboard, with a little tinkering"—he pointed to a tiny jet attached to the base of the board—"provided the acceleration necessary to get me back here."

"And you've come to take Sheila home," Darian said in a hard voice.

"Oh, I am sorry, but no. There's simply not enough power on this skateboard."

"It figures," Sheila murmured.

"I'm working on it," the scientist said with a frown. "However, we'll deal with that problem when the time comes. I'm here on another matter entirely. When I left you last time, I had every intention of materializing in my laboratory. But I took a slight detour and wound up in the camp of that character you call Nemor. He certainly is a charismatic fellow. His followers think the world of him. But he's making plans that could be dangerous. Very dangerous indeed."

"You mean for the unicorn riders," Sheila said.

For once Dr. Reit gave a straightforward answer. "Sheila, I overheard a conversation between Nemor and a man named Valan, a man who fancies himself a wizard. Wears a gold necklace."

"He *is* a wizard," Darian said. "And a powerful one."

"Anyway, it became clear from their conversation that Nemor is not fighting Dynasian at all. Oh, I think he did for a while, but the tyrant has bought him back. The attack on the fortress you told me about is Dynasian's plan. He means not only to lure Illyria into his stronghold, but to destroy all of the riders as well. They said something about 'natural defenses,' but I couldn't quite catch their meaning. Perhaps I should return and investigate further. That will mean, of course, that I will have to recalculate my coordinates from here and—"

"It's a trap," Darian said quietly. "And even now my sister rides into the traitor's camp." Using the trees for support, he raised himself slowly and then stood for a moment, as if to be sure he had his balance back. He gave a soft, low whistle.

"Darian," Sheila said uneasily, "what are you doing?"

Darian ignored her question, instead turning to Dr. Reit. "The Sareen encampment, did you notice where it was—hidden by trees, in a valley, on a hillside?"

"Dear me"—the scientist's form began to waver—"I didn't really look. I was so absorbed in what Nemor and Valan were saying, not to mention my own coordinates of velocity and—" As he spoke his image gradually began to fade until by the time he said the word *velocity*, he was no more than a voice.

"Bye, Dr. Reit." Sheila tried not to sound hurt. She knew the scientist was doing his best to rescue her, but every time he left, she couldn't help wondering if he had left for good.

Darian took her mind off her problems by whistling again, this time a little louder. In answer, Wildwing ran toward them, clearly excited by the summons. Darian turned toward his tent.

"Darian," Sheila said, "where do you think you're going?"

"I'm going to get my saddle," he said casually. "Where did you think I was going?"

Sheila sighed. "You're in no shape to ride Wildwing. Pelu said you were to rest."

"Pelu didn't know that Nemor is fighting for Dynasian. I can't let Illyria ride into his camp without warning. And as for riding Wildwing, that won't be a problem."

"With one arm?" Sheila scoffed.

The boy shrugged and disappeared into his tent. He emerged a few moments later, holding both saddle and sword in one hand. Sheila watched with mixed feelings. She couldn't help but admire how well he was managing. At the same time he was taking a serious risk. After all, it wasn't like his arm was in a plaster cast; one good jolt on Wildwing could easily disturb the newly set bones.

And after last night, she knew she couldn't stand to see him in pain again.

"Riding with my arm in a sling isn't that different from riding with a spear," Darian said reasonably. He fitted the saddle over the unicorn's back. "Besides, you're going to be the one riding him. Then all I have to do is hold on."

"You're out of your mind," Sheila said. "We can't leave Quiet Storm."

"We're leaving Quiet Storm guarded by the other unicorns. They're certainly better protection than either one of us. Besides, do you really think anyone could get near him in the state he's in?"

Quiet Storm was no longer bucking, but his head was lowered, his horn tearing violently through the air. Clearly, he was still in the midst of some invisible battle.

"Valan got near him last night," Sheila pointed out.

Awkwardly, Darian struggled to buckle his sword around his waist. Sheila didn't offer to help.

"Look," he said, "I don't feel good about leaving him, either, but I think I can do more good by warning Illyria than by watching Quiet Storm wear himself out."

"Fine. You go."

"Oh, no. I'm not leaving you alone."

Sheila faced him furiously. "I don't need your protection!"

"But I need yours," he said with a disarming grin. His eyes went wide with calculated innocence. "Didn't Illyria say you were supposed to take care of me?"

"She didn't tell me it would be like babysitting for a hyperactive toddler!" Sheila crossed her arms and turned away from him. Briefly she wondered if the word *hyperactive* had translated into his language.

Even with one arm in a sling, Darian mounted the unicorn easily. His pressed his knee against Wildwing's side, and the unicorn walked around Sheila so that Darian was once again facing her. He held out his left hand. "Please?"

"You'll go anyway, won't you?"

"I have to."

Sheila gave in with a groan and let him pull her into the saddle. "All right," she said, "but if anyone asks, this was *your* idea."

9

Valan's Deal

Neither Darian nor Sheila knew exactly where Odelia was, but Darian had the general idea that it was about twelve miles northwest of the canyon. He was sure that once they reached Odelia, someone would tell them where to find the Sareen camp.

Sheila didn't have a better idea, so she followed his directions. She just hoped that they wouldn't encounter any of Dynasian's soldiers. The two of them alone, especially with Darian wounded, wouldn't stand a chance.

The noon sun burned hot as they rode, and Sheila leaned forward into the wind. The air was so hot and dry, it felt as if they were riding under a blow dryer. *Why,* Sheila wondered, *couldn't she have time traveled into a world where people did things like go to the beach?*

Darian broke into her thoughts as they came to a fork in the road. "I think you want to go right here."

"You *think?*"

"Just try it."

Darian hadn't said much since they had left camp. He had been too busy holding on and trying to keep his arm from being jostled. On a horse they wouldn't have gotten ten yards. But Wildwing moved with the near-psychic intuition Sheila had come to identify with the unicorns. The powerful stallion held himself in a smooth, even canter that was as close as he could come to cushioning his riders.

"To the *right*," Darian repeated in a tight voice.

Sheila wondered if he was in pain or just anxious about Illyria. Using her knee, she guided Wildwing to the right.

Ahead, the narrow road dipped down sharply, and as far as Sheila could tell, it was completely overgrown with a canopy of trees. In the dry southern lands of the empire, this was definitely weird. She half-expected Wildwing to turn and run in the opposite direction.

"Darian"—she tried to keep her voice calm—"are you sure this is the way we want to go?"

He leaned forward in the saddle, peering over her shoulder. "Keep going," he said quietly.

Wildwing walked at a steady, even pace, carrying them into what looked like a tunnel formed by the trees. A few narrow bands of sunlight slipped through the thick cover of branches. And yet there was no relief from the heat. If anything, it was hotter under the trees—and incredibly humid. Sheila brushed a soft green frond away from her face. The farther they went, the thicker the trees grew and the darker the road became. What had they done, suddenly ridden into the heart of a jungle?

"Darian," Sheila said, "I think we took a wrong turn."

"No, we didn't."

With considerable effort, she got Wildwing to halt. "Look at this place—all these trees. I haven't seen anything like this since I entered your world. It's all wrong for this climate."

Darian's voice was sharp with impatience. "Don't you think I know that?"

"Well, if you know it, why are we here?" Sheila tugged

on the straps of her backpack. Beneath it, her tunic was soaked with sweat. Even the air was changed on this overgrown path. The air reeked with the smell of something sweet and decaying. Whatever this place was, it felt completely wrong.

Sheila made a quick decision. She wasn't going to argue with Darian on this one. She pressed her heels into Wildwing and brought his head around.

The unicorn looked at her for a moment, brought his head back, and remained exactly where he was. When she tried again to turn him, he walked forward deeper into the trees. Sheila felt her chest tighten with panic.

Darian leaned forward. "Keep going."

This time she brought Wildwing to a dead stop. "Darian, the land can't possibly be like this. Not when it was so dry just a little ways back."

"I know."

Sheila's voice rose higher than she meant it to. "I thought you were the one who didn't approve of riding straight into traps. What do you think we're doing now?"

Darian pressed his heels into Wildwing, and the stallion moved forward. Above them the thick cover of trees completely blocked sun and sky.

Sheila tried to keep her voice light but couldn't stop it from shaking. "This is worse than riding at night. I can't see at all."

"But Wildwing can." Darian gave her shoulders a quick squeeze. "We've got to trust him."

Sheila wound her fingers even more tightly through the black mane. She was holding on so hard she was sure her fingers would be cramped forever.

"There!" Darian's arm shot forward, pointing to a small point of red light blazing in the darkness.

The unicorn stopped, and Sheila felt him tense beneath her.

Ahead of them the point of light became larger—a small red orb spinning furiously in the darkness.

Oh, Dr. Reit, Sheila thought, *you never told me about anything like this.*

As they watched the light spin closer Sheila could see that it was not just a circle of red light, but red light racing in a geometric sunlike pattern. It was the *krino.*

Darian must have recognized it at the same moment Sheila did. She heard the metallic scrape of his sword being drawn.

"So you want to finish what you started last night?" There was a dry, hoarse laugh. Then the light spun out into the long lines of a man's form, and Valan, Nemor's mage, stood before them. His voice was mocking as he addressed Darian. "It is useless, you know. You've left Quiet Storm to die unprotected, and all for nothing. This time I will not be gentle with you," he promised with an evil laugh. "This time you will suffer more than a broken arm."

Sheila didn't know where she found the courage to speak, but when she did she was amazed to discover her voice no longer shook. "What do you want from us?"

Thin streaks of red light danced around Valan's form. Dr. Reit had often said that everyone gave off a certain level of energy. He even claimed his cat Einstein gave off the most calming energy he had ever encountered. It occurred to Sheila that she was watching Valan's energy, and it was anything but calming.

"I think," Valan said, "that the question should be turned around. After all, it was *you* who came to me this time."

"We don't want anything from you," Sheila replied.

"That's not true," Darian said quietly. "I did seek you. I want to know where my sister is. And I want your word that you won't use your power against her. We'll match Nemor, force against force, but no magic."

Valan laughed again, thin lines of red light darting into the treetops. Sheila was surprised nothing caught fire. "You know what this entails, young one," he taunted. "If you want my help, you'll have to pay."

Darian's breath caught, almost as if he was choking back a sob. "You want the unicorn."

"That's part of it, but not all. You can't buy magic that cheaply."

Sheila turned to see Darian sheathing his sword. "No!" she cried.

"Be quiet!" he snapped. To Valan he called, "The girl didn't know anything about this. Let her go and you can have your price."

The mage considered the proposition, the light about him growing more and more frantic. *He's calling up more energy,* Sheila realized. *He's getting ready to cast a spell.*

"The girl goes," he agreed at last. "She will leave you here. And she'll not get over it easily."

"I'm not going anywhere," Sheila told them both.

Darian's hand closed over her arm, gripping it so tightly it hurt. "You're going to get off Wildwing and walk out of here," he whispered fiercely. "Walk back the way we came in and don't look back."

"Stop giving me orders!" Sheila hissed. She turned away from him, concentrating instead on Valan. What was he going to do to Darian and Wildwing? And what made Darian think he would keep his word once they had paid his price? He would probably kill Wildwing and Darian, and then he would finish off Illyria and the riders. There *had* to be a way to fight the mage.

"Sheila." Darian's voice held a dangerous note of warning. If she hadn't been so terrified of Valan, it might have scared her. He swore furiously under his breath. "Do as I tell you. Now!"

And then Sheila had an idea. It might not work at all, but it was worth trying. "All right," she said to Darian. "I'll go, but since I may not see you again—" Her voice broke. She couldn't help it. If she was wrong, she never *would* see him again. "I want to give you something." She slipped the pack off her back and unzipped it.

The mage's voice cut through the darkness. "You've wasted too much time, girl. I can no longer let you go."

Three things happened at once. The first was not unexpected: Darian drew his sword. The second was a little more unusual: The streaks of light that flickered around Valan drew together in the burning red configuration of the *krino* and shot toward Sheila and Darian. And the third thing that happened was somewhere between a miracle and sheer luck: Sheila grabbed the mirror from her pack and held it up like a shield to the burning red light that was streaking toward them. There was a flash as the light met the mirror, bounced off it, and ricocheted backward. A bloodcurdling cry split the air, and then everything went dark.

For a long moment no one moved. Even the unicorn barely breathed.

"The *krino*'s gone," Darian said at last. "And so is Valan . . . isn't he?"

Wildwing answered by snorting his agreement and walking past the spot where the mage had stood.

Still shaken, Sheila didn't answer. But the sweet, decaying scent was gone, and she knew that they were safe. At least for now.

10

Lightning

Wildwing stepped calmly out of the tree-covered valley
where Sheila and Darian had confronted Valan. Beyond
the tree line the sun was shining as brightly as ever. Sheila
was actually happy to see the scorched landscape again.

She turned in the saddle. Behind her Darian sat looking unusually pale.

"Are you all right?" she asked.

He nodded his head.

"How about your arm?"

"I'm fine." He smiled, but his eyes were dark and serious. "You defeated a mage today. And you saved my life.
Again. I'm indebted to you, Sheila McCarthy." He ran
his hand lightly through her hair. "I think you must be a
sorceress after all."

"You know I'm not," Sheila said quietly. She still felt
shaken by the encounter. She would probably have night-
mares about Valan for the rest of her life. And something
he had said was bothering her.

Darian made a clicking sound with his tongue, and the
unicorn began to move forward at a gentle walk. Sheila
turned around quickly to grab a handful of mane.

"Darian, do you remember what Valan said about
Quiet Storm?"

His reply was barely audible. "That we left him to die unprotected."

"We've got to go back to the camp," Sheila said. "Maybe it's not too late."

"And maybe it is." Darian's voice was drained of all emotion. "We've got to find the Sareen encampment and warn Illyria."

"No!" Sheila brought Wildwing to a halt. She turned to face Darian, who was looking at her as if she had lost her mind. "It's not that I don't care about Illyria," she explained, "but Illyria's got six riders with her and is very capable of taking care of herself."

Darian stared at her, unbelieving. "In case you don't remember," he said, "Illyria and that overwhelming company of six riders are about to be betrayed."

"I know that. But Darian, I can't stand the thought of Quiet Storm dying because we abandoned him. We've got to at least try and save him. Then we can ride to Odelia."

Darian's eyes were hard with barely controlled anger, and Sheila knew that she was about to be overruled. And with a sense of desperation, she also knew that this time Darian was wrong and she couldn't let that happen.

"You just told me you were indebted to me," she said quickly. "If you really mean that, then I'm calling in the debt."

"What?"

"I saved your life," she said. "Twice. But we'll call it even if you just do this one thing for me—we go back to the camp now."

For a long moment Darian stared at her. Sheila knew she was asking him to make an impossible choice. She was pitting his love for his sister against the warriors' unbreakable code of honor. And she was counting on the fact that like Illyria and the other riders, he would not be able to go back on his word, not when he had given it in thanks for his life.

"All right," he said at last. "We go back to attend to Quiet Storm, but if anything happens to Illyria—"

Sheila turned before he could complete the threat, and dug her heels into Wildwing's side. She would worry about the consequences of her decision later. Right now the only thing that mattered was getting to Quiet Storm.

Dusk was falling when Wildwing reached the mouth of the canyon. As fast as the stallion was, this time he hadn't been fast enough for Sheila. She leapt from the unicorn's back and raced into the riders' camp.

"He's still alive!" she called to Darian. She thought she would collapse from relief.

The silver unicorn stood alone at the far end of the canyon. He was no longer fighting his invisible opponent, but standing quietly with an odd, expectant air. *He's probably waiting for Illyria*, Sheila thought.

"He looks better, don't you think?" she asked Darian, who had walked Wildwing into the canyon, cooling him down. "He's much calmer. Maybe Valan was just bluffing. Or maybe we broke his spell back there."

"Stay here," Darian said. Slowly he approached the unicorn. "Quiet Storm," he called softly. "Will you let an old friend say hello?"

The unicorn watched warily as the boy advanced.

Darian had gotten within about ten yards of him when Quiet Storm began to rake the air with his horn. "Shhh," the boy said in a soothing voice. "It's all right. I'm not going to hurt you. I only want to take a look at you."

Quiet Storm began to buck with a frenzy, and Darian quickly retreated. He turned to Sheila with a look of resignation. "I guess that just because Valan's gone doesn't mean his magic is."

"Do you think Quiet Storm is worse?"

"I don't know. The only thing that's certain is that he's still bound by magic." Darian put a hand on Sheila's shoulder. "Come on, let's get something to eat, and then we can figure out a way to feed Quiet Storm without getting too close."

The camp seemed unnaturally quiet as they worked to build a fire and heat the broth that Pelu had left for Darian. The night had fallen quickly, and Quiet Storm stood in a wash of moonlight, nearly motionless. Did that mean the spell was winning, since the unicorn no longer had the strength to fight it?

Sheila felt helpless. If she had really destroyed Valan, why was his spell still controlling the unicorn? Was the mage right—was Quiet Storm really dying? And if he was, what could Sheila do to stop it? She wished Illyria and Pelu were with them, and she was beginning to wish that she had gone to warn them.

"Here." Darian handed her a bowl of steaming broth.

She set it down without bothering to taste it. For the first time it occurred to Sheila that the others might not come back. Not ever. *Stop it,* she told herself fiercely. *Thinking like that won't help.*

Darian wasn't eating, either. He used his spoon to dig a shallow hole in the ground. "I wonder where they are now," he said. "If what your Dr. Reit told us was right, then they're probably safe until they actually attack the fortress. After all, Nemor won't ruin his own trap. The only problem is we don't know when the attack will take place."

"Maybe Illyria's—" began Sheila.

At the mention of Illyria's name Quiet Storm whinnied loudly and began to pace anxiously.

"He's worried, too," Darian said grimly. Then his head came up sharply and he pointed to Quiet Storm in amazement.

The unicorn had reared up on his two hind legs and now stood as if suspended in the air, his head cocked toward the back of the canyon. With a loud snort, Quiet Storm brought his forelegs down. He gave a last powerful buck and then tore toward the back of the canyon.

"What's he doing?" Sheila said. "There's only rock back there."

Darian didn't answer. He took off after the unicorn. Sheila was right behind him. Maybe the stallion really was going crazy. She had heard of "loco" horses, who tried to buck their way through walls. Was Quiet Storm going to try to tear through a wall of solid rock?

Ahead of her she heard Darian cry out. Quiet Storm had broken into a wild, headlong gallop. And each time his hoofs struck the ground, a blazing white light flashed up.

Moonlight met the unicorn's own lightning as the animal reached the end of the canyon. For a second the stallion paused, and the sight made Sheila dizzy with wonder. Quiet Storm stood bathed in light, his silver horn gleaming. Suddenly there was a tremendous flash as a bolt of lightning ripped into the hard rock wall. Sheila covered her ears to keep from being deafened by the terrific thunderclap that followed. Then it was quiet again. Quiet Storm gave a triumphant whinny as he galloped through a narrow pass, freshly cut into the canyon wall.

In unspoken agreement Sheila and Darian went after the unicorn despite the fact that they had no hope of keeping up with him. Illyria had once said that Quiet Storm could outrun the wind if he wanted to, and it wasn't an idle boast. Still, they couldn't just watch him disappear.

The pass through the canyon led to a narrow shelf of land that wound up behind the canyon walls. It meant running nearly straight uphill, and both Sheila and Darian were gasping for breath by the time they reached the top.

They stood for a minute, trying to control their breathing. Sheila peered around. It looked like they had come out of the canyon and entered—an olive grove? A full moon illuminated the landscape. The land was flat as far as she could see. There were no houses or buildings, just thick, gnarled olive trees, growing in what might have a long time ago been rows. The trees themselves were spaced far apart with only a sparse covering of grass on the ground. There was no sign of Quiet Storm, but if he was still in the grove, sooner or later they would be able to see him.

Darian caught his breath first. "I don't even know what direction to go in," he admitted.

"Where are we?" Sheila asked. "I didn't see this grove today, or when I went into Ansar."

"No, I didn't, either. But look at the size of these trees—they're ancient. All of them. They've been here forever."

Something about Darian's tone made Sheila shiver. *Stop imagining things,* she told herself. *You've seen old trees before. How about the redwoods in California?* But it wasn't just the trees. It was the feeling that they had stumbled into a place that had been unchanged for thousands of years, unchanged for a reason.

A sudden flash of white light blazed through the grove. "There he is!" Darian cried, and they were off again.

They ran for what seemed hours, and only rarely did they catch a glimpse of the silver unicorn. What they saw was the lightning he struck from the ground. It was almost as if Quiet Storm *wanted* them to follow him through the ancient grove, the grove that never seemed to end.

At last there came a point when Sheila and Darian

thought they had lost Quiet Storm. It had been a long time since they had seen either the unicorn or the lightning.

Sheila slowed down and bent over, hands on knees, taking in deep gulps of the night air. "What are we chasing anyway?" she asked when her heart had slowed to an almost normal pace. "I mean, I'm beginning to think Quiet Storm isn't here at all." She looked up at Darian, unable to hide the fear in her eyes. "What if we've been chasing some sort of illusion. You know this grove is . . . is . . ."

"Magic," he said, letting the word hang between them. "I'm not sure whose or what kind, but you're right. It's a place of power."

"No," Sheila was almost pleading, "not after what happened with Valan." She stood up and wrapped her arms around her, as if for comfort. "Not again."

"I don't think it's quite the same," Darian said in a thoughtful tone.

A thin mist was rising from the ground. Quiet Storm was gone, and they were alone in a place that reeked of magic. The quiet was unbearable.

"What do we do now?" Sheila asked, not really expecting an answer.

The answer came from Quiet Storm. There was a blinding flash of light so bright that both Darian and Sheila covered their eyes. Then Quiet Storm stood before them as he had at the end of the canyon, bathed in the mingled rays of moonlight and the light he drew from the ground. The unicorn was staring intently into a pool of dark water. Then, as if suddenly aware that he had company, he lifted his head and looked straight at them with a clear, regal gaze.

"Come on." Darian took Sheila's hand. "I think he's waiting for us."

11

❧ ❖ ❧

The Scrying Pool

Slowly Sheila and Darian approached Quiet Storm. This time the unicorn showed no sign of bolting. He stood calmly, waiting for them.

"Hey, Quiet Storm." Sheila held out her hand, but the unicorn brushed her off impatiently. He stood staring down into the pool of black water at his feet.

The pond was small; it couldn't have been more than six feet across. The full moon was reflected neatly in its center, and the strange thing was that the mist that rose from the ground didn't touch the pond at all. Its surface was perfectly clear. There was only black water framing a glowing, silver moon.

With a soft whinny Quiet Storm dipped his horn into the water. Sheila knew that unicorns were water conners—if they dipped their horns into water—even poisoned water—it became pure at once. Did Quiet Storm want them to drink from the pond?

Suddenly the surface of the pond began to cloud over. Sheila looked up quickly. The skies were clear; it wasn't a reflection. But an image was being formed in the water.

Darian sank to his knees, cradling his broken arm. "Illyria?" His voice was a hoarse whisper.

Sheila knelt beside him. The reflection of the moon had disappeared. In its place was a startlingly clear picture of Illyria entering a tent. Nemor followed close behind her. Illyria looked irritated and Nemor, exasperated. Sheila had a hunch that they were not getting along.

"I know you don't trust me," Nemor was saying, "but perhaps this will convince you of my intent." He crossed the tent, took a roll of parchment from the corner, and carefully opened it on a broad wooden table.

"Stars above!" Darian swore. They were staring at a detailed drawing of a mountain whose top had been leveled. A steep road had been cut into the side that faced the city of Ansar. What couldn't be seen from the city was the huge stone fortress that had been built on the mountaintop. Like the city, the fortress was surrounded by a stone wall.

Nemor pointed to the top of the wall. "There are guards posted here and here and here. No one can get up that road without being seen."

"You said there was another route," Illyria reminded him.

Nemor unrolled a second drawing. This one showed the side of the mountain that faced away from Ansar.

Sheila stared at it, puzzled. Although the drawing was detailed, all she saw was the side of a mountain with craggy and smooth rocks. She did not see anything that resembled a path.

"Here." Nemor's finger traced a line that ran up the steepest part of the mountain. "It's not what you'd call a road. It may not even qualify as a path, but it will get me up undetected and it's close to this gate. Once I'm inside the wall, I'll throw open the western gate, the one that opens to the road, to the Sareen and you and your riders. Then it's only a matter of a good, strong attack."

"Then it's only a matter of Dynasian destroying you," Darian translated. "I can't stand watching her agree to this."

"She has to free the unicorns," Sheila said, knowing that Illyria would not refuse a way into the fortress.

The Unicorn Queen studied the map with interest. "How do you plan to get over the wall?"

Nemor's voice was soft and chilling. "Treachery . . . I've planted my men among Dynasian's. They will help me."

"You mean *us*." Illyria nearly laughed as his eyes widened in astonishment. They were the color of amber, eyes like a lion's. "I'm not asking my riders to attack Dynasian's fortress unless I can personally guarantee that the gates will be open for them. If you want our help, you'll have to take me with you."

"He's going to kill her," Darian said. "And she's making it easy for him. All he has to do is push her off when they're climbing. Or give her to the soldiers on the wall. Or—"

"Sshhh!" Sheila cut him off as Illyria asked a short question: "When?"

Nemor's answer took them all by surprise. "Tomorrow. The longer we wait, the longer Dynasian has to uncover our plan. We'll start the climb before sunrise—the heat makes it impossible during the day. Given the time it will take us to get up the mountain, we should have our troops attack at midday."

"Tomorrow?" Sheila echoed hollowly. "How will we ever get to her in time?"

Darian groaned, and the mist that had not touched the pond now floated across its surface in a gauzy cloud. It cleared a few moments later and left only the reflection of the full, white moon floating in the still black water.

Sheila put a hand on Darian's shoulder and tried to think of something comforting to say. She noticed that neither she nor Darian nor Quiet Storm were reflected in the water, and the strangeness of it unnerved her. What was it they had just seen—the past, the future, or the present? And was it even real? In this world it could easily be just another illusion, one of Valan's tricks. Clearly, they had seen what they were meant to see. Now she wanted to get out of this place fast.

She stood up and ran her hand along Quiet Storm's flank. "Will you take us to Illyria?" she asked.

Quiet Storm whipped his head away with an angry snort.

"I think he just refused," Sheila said.

Darian stood up. "He probably doesn't know how to get out of this place, either." He turned slowly. "It's the same in every direction. Just more trees. And it goes on for miles. You'd have to be a bird to find a way out."

"Darian"—Sheila's voice suddenly filled with a wild hope—"I think our way out just arrived." Against the moonlit sky she could make out a flock of eagles swooping down through the grove. They flew in a broad V formation, each bird the size of a man.

Quiet Storm lifted his head and called out in greeting, which was immediately returned by the eagle that flew at the head of the group.

They settled on the edge of the pond. In the light of the full moon there was a stirring of the great wings and then their bodies blurred. If Sheila hadn't seen the transformation once before, she would have thought it a trick of the moonlight and mist. But the eagles were gone, and she and Darian were now staring at a band of stalwart warriors clad for battle.

A fierce-eyed young man, his long, black hair held back by a silver circlet, stepped out from the mist and laid a hand on the unicorn's neck.

Quiet Storm gave a nervous whinny.

"I know," the man said soothingly, "and I will help you. I promise."

He turned to Sheila and Darian. "It has been a long time, my friends."

Sheila thought she would collapse with relief. The handsome warrior who stood before them was Laric, prince of Perian, and Illyria's love.

"Laric?" Darian sounded as if he was sure he was hallucinating.

"One and the same." The prince made a sweeping gesture with his red cloak. "You are welcome in this grove." He frowned at the two teenagers before him. "Though I would dearly love to know how you found it."

Sheila opened her mouth to explain, but Laric shook his head. "You can tell me later. Neither of you is going anywhere until Quiet Storm is free of the spell that holds him, and—"

"But Illyria's in danger!" Darian broke in angrily.

"I know that," Laric said with a sigh. "Believe me, if we are to help her, we will need Quiet Storm with us." He gave the unicorn a worried look. "He came here for help, and I will do what I can, but the spell that binds him is a powerful one. He's just lucky it was never completed. Something must have interrupted whoever cast it."

"Some*one*," Sheila said. "It was Darian."

Laric's eyes traveled to the boy's splinted arm. "And that was your payment?"

Darian nodded.

"Well, perhaps I can do something about that, too," Laric said. "But first, let me work on Quiet Storm."

Laric led the unicorn to a spot at the center point of four great trees and began an incantation.

Sheila and Darian waited with Laric's men. Sheila's eyes never left Laric. He was without question the most gorgeous man she had ever seen. *When* he was a man, that is. She wondered how Illyria could bear being in love with a man cursed to live in another form.

The prince raised his left hand and traced a circle around the unicorn's head, then another around the gleaming silver horn. All the while he spoke words of magic. After what seemed like an eternity to Sheila, Laric left the unicorn and came to sit beside her.

"So," he said, "how have you been, traveler from another world?"

Sheila blushed furiously. "Fine," she said.

"But your queen is not. Tell me what happened."

So Sheila told him all that had gone on and what she and Darian had just seen in the pond.

Laric listened silently as she poured out the whole story, but Sheila could feel him tense with fury.

"This is worse than I guessed," he said, getting to his feet. "We must go to her at once, but there is the matter of the spells. . . . Quiet Storm is not yet free, and to reach Illyria in time, I will have to lay a spell of my own on him. And I cannot do that until Valan's magic is gone." He gazed up at the full moon and sighed. "And all this before sunrise."

"Then what we saw in the pond was real?" Sheila asked. "Not just some illusion?"

"First of all," Laric said dryly, "it is not a pond. It is a scrying pool. Secondly, scrying pools are not capable of illusion. They reveal visions of reality to those who are ready for them. You may trust it completely."

He turned toward Darian. "Come. We must heal your arm. At least I will not waste the time we have."

Sheila watched as Laric carefully loosened the sling and removed the splint from Darian's arm. Gently he felt the break. "It's been skillfully set," he said. "Now we must ask it to knit faster." Holding Darian's arm between his hands, he murmured words in a language Sheila had never heard before.

Darian watched curiously.

"There will be some pain," said the prince, "but it will not last. Don't move your arm."

As Laric spoke Darian's face whitened and he shut his eyes. Sheila slipped her hand into his, and he clenched it so tightly she thought she might need to be healed as well.

"There." Laric released Darian's arm. He, too, was pale. "Now, turn your wrist. . . . "

On Laric's instructions Darian moved his arm through a series of exercises, the expression on his face changing from doubt to wonder to sheer delight.

"Yes, it will do," said Laric gruffly. "But don't tackle any more mages if you can possibly avoid it."

Darian's grin faded. "What you just did . . . that was no ordinary healing. You are a mage as well?" Though phrased as a question, it was a statement.

Laric shrugged. "Perian is not like your country. There, everyone is taught magic from childhood. And since I was raised in the palace, I was taught a bit more than others. Among your people it may be impressive. In my own land I am far from the rank of a true mage." He gave a bitter laugh. "And the proof is that I am unable to break Mardock's curse."

"But you brought Quiet Storm to Illyria," Sheila said. No matter what Laric thought, the coming of the unicorns was impressive.

The prince smiled. "I like unicorns," he said simply. "Illyria saved my life, and I didn't know if I'd ever see her again. Quiet Storm was the best gift I could leave her. And now I should see to him so I can send him back."

"Wait," Darian said. "Just one more thing. This grove . . . what is it?"

Laric hesitated, as if he wasn't sure he should answer.

"Yesterday we rode past the end of the canyon," Sheila said. "And yesterday there wasn't an olive grove here."

"This grove has nothing to do with time or place," Laric answered. "It does not lie within Dynasian's empire. And that's all I can tell you." He smiled and brushed a strand of auburn hair out of her eyes. "You should be used to strange travels by now, child of another time."

One of Laric's men joined them. "We've prepared places for you two to sleep," he said. "You will only have time for a nap, but Laric will be awhile with Quiet Storm and you should get what rest you can."

When Sheila turned for a last glimpse of Laric, she saw him working over Quiet Storm, both of them glowing in a haze of white light.

Sheila dreamed of Morning Star. She dreamed that Morning Star stood at the side of the scrying pool and dipped her black horn into its smooth depths. The pool began to cloud over . . . and Sheila sat upright, shaking herself awake. If it was possible to receive a message in your dreams, she was sure that Morning Star was trying to tell her to go to the scrying pool.

Most of Laric's men were sleeping and she didn't want to wake them. But she did wake Darian, and together they returned to the edge of the pool. Morning Star was, of course, nowhere in sight. But the pool was clouded over, as it had been in her dream.

At first they didn't recognize the image that formed in the black water, for the scene that was revealed was very dark.

"It's the mountain," Darian said. "Dynasian's mountain."

The wind caused the surface of the pool to ripple, and then Sheila and Darian could make out two human forms in the night, looking impossibly small against the massive wall of rock.

"Illyria and Nemor," said Laric, coming to stand beside them. "And it is dark on the mountain, as it is here. We are seeing the present."

They saw Nemor leading Illyria up the wall. Nemor moved up the steep rock face as surely as if he had climbed it a thousand times. He never placed a foot or hand awkwardly. Illyria followed, not quite as adept, but easily holding her own.

Laric studied the image and drew a sharp breath. "He wears the *krino*," he said. "And there is something else. Do you see the way he moves—he has the lion's energy."

Sheila had always thought Nemor looked somewhat leonine, and it made him all the more attractive. "So?" she asked.

"Throughout time the lion and the unicorn have been deadly enemies," Laric answered. "When they meet, only one of them will survive. Dynasian could have not chosen a more lethal agent."

And yet, for all the danger she was in, Illyria seemed to be doing rather well. Though the wall of rock grew increasingly steep, she followed Nemor without hesitation. About halfway up, they stood together on a ledge that Sheila figured was all of four inches wide.

The rebel leader turned to Illyria and put a hand under her chin. "You are very beautiful, Lady," he said softly.

Sheila thought she saw compassion in his eyes. "Are you sure you want to continue?"

Illyria shook off his touch. "I said that I would enter the fortress with you. I don't go back on my word. Do you?"

His voice was gentle when he answered. "I did not ask you to make this climb. There would be no disgrace in changing your mind."

"Do you want me to lead the way?" Illyria asked mockingly.

Nemor growled something unintelligible and moved on.

Sheila, Darian, and Laric watched, fascinated and helpless.

The full moon paled and the sun rose, and still Nemor and Illyria climbed. Soon the top of the mountain was in sight.

"Sunrise," Laric said, pulling himself away from the vision in the scrying pool. "Quiet Storm should be ready for you now."

Quiet Storm stood at the center of the four trees, looking calm and attentive. He nuzzled Laric affectionately as the prince laid a hand on his neck.

"You've cured him," Sheila said.

Laric smiled wearily. "That and a little more. Get on, both of you. He will take you to Illyria."

"He'll know how to get us out of this place?" Sheila asked uncertainly. In the gray dawn light the grove seemed to go on endlessly in all directions. Wherever she looked she saw only the thick, gnarled trees and, between them, wide stretches of grass.

It was Darian who answered. "That's Quiet Storm's gift. He always knows exactly where to go."

"He will bring you safely to Illyria," Laric agreed, "but

you must leave now, for the journey from this place is a long one. . . . And you will not be traveling as you expect." He murmured a few words of enchantment to the unicorn.

Sheila and Darian watched open-mouthed as Quiet Storm lifted his front legs and leaped upward into the air. He didn't come down. He ran above them, frisking like a young colt, his silver cloven hoofs darting in and out of the treetops.

"That's enough," Laric said sternly.

The unicorn returned to earth at once, looking not at all chastened.

"Get on," the prince urged them. "We will follow you."

Darian mounted first, then Sheila in front of him. Both were too surprised to say anything at all. Laric spoke a few more words to the unicorn, and then Quiet Storm leaped into the air and flew straight toward the sunrise.

12

✂ ❖ ✂
The Siege

Quiet Storm ran on the wind, his hoofs leaving faint silver streaks against the sky, his mane streaming out behind him. Sheila held on, awed by the dizzying landscape below. At first there had been endless miles of the ancient trees, as if the olive grove were a country unto itself. Then, when the sun was nearly at its zenith, there was a flash of light so bright that both Darian and Sheila had to shut their eyes. When they opened them again, the grove was gone and they were soaring over the city of Ansar. Behind them the eagles flew, a fierce winged guard.

Sheila suppressed a shiver as they neared Dynasian's mountain. It seemed as if the mountain lay in wait for them. One of the eagles darted below Quiet Storm's hoofs and ahead. Tracing the bird's flight, Sheila saw that the eagle was calling to a small band of warriors galloping down the road that led to the mountain.

"There are the riders!" she called to Darian above the sound of the wind.

There was no sign of the Sareen, but the riders were on their way to the fortress with the wild unicorns behind them. Sheila knew that they would soon be climbing the road that wound up the mountain—exactly as Nemor had planned.

Quiet Storm turned, heading for the other side of the mountain, the side that Illyria and Nemor had scaled. Sheila looked desperately for a sign of the Unicorn Queen. Was it possible that she and Nemor were still climbing?

"There!" Darian called.

Quiet Storm hovered in the air above the scene. Nemor stood just inside the surrounding wall, looking up at Illyria, who crouched on its top. Obviously, they had just reached the top of the mountain and were about to enter the fortress.

Sheila held her breath as Illyria dropped from the top of the wall to stand beside Nemor. She could see them talking, and then there was a flash of bright metal and Illyria was behind Nemor, her knife drawn across his throat. Without protest Nemor began to walk toward the fortress.

"Don't go inside!" Sheila screamed. "It's a trap!"

"She can't hear you. We're too far away!" Darian said furiously as a door in the fortress opened and Illyria and Nemor vanished inside. "Can't you make Quiet Storm land?"

Sheila knew how to get a unicorn to walk, canter, or gallop, but she couldn't imagine what signal she was supposed to use to make Quiet Storm start his descent. She pressed her knees and heels against his sides. She tugged on his mane. She leaned forward and explained exactly what she wanted him to do. The unicorn gave no sign of understanding.

Darian saw what was happening at once. "Never mind," he said gently. "He's not going anywhere until he's ready. I guess we've just got to be patient."

Since they were no longer moving forward, the sound of the wind rushing past had vanished. The sun was blazing and the air was hot and deathly still. Dynasian's soldiers marched in silent parade along the top of the fortress walls. It was a small comfort that when Illyria had entered the fortress Nemor had been her captive.

"I wish I knew what Dynasian has planned," Darian said restlessly. "What was that Dr. Reit said—something about 'natural defenses'?"

"Yeah, but even Dr. Reit didn't know what Nemor meant," Sheila answered.

Since there was nothing else to do, she studied the scene below. The iron gate facing the road was open for the approaching riders, Sheila realized with a sinking sensation. The gate led into a wide, square courtyard, surrounded by thick outer walls and facing the front of the fortress. Like the mountain itself, the fortress and its walls were carved of a pale—almost white—rock that seemed to shimmer in the midday sun. Dynasian's fortress was immense. Sheila figured it had to be at least four stories high and big enough to cover an entire city block.

One of the eagles cried out in alarm as a door to the roof of the fortress suddenly opened, and Illyria was pushed out, her hands bound behind her back. Two soldiers followed and pulled her to the very edge of the ramparts overlooking the courtyard.

Then, from the other side of the ramparts, a carved stone door opened and a short, fat man dressed in gaudy robes emerged. Sheila would have recognized him anywhere. It was Dynasian himself. And Nemor was at his side.

Sheila tried to call out, hoping the sight of a flying unicorn would at least distract Dynasian, but her voice was paralyzed by the panic that gripped her. She felt Darian's arm around her, and then Quiet Storm and the eagles began to descend, dropping silently through the air toward the fortress below.

The unicorn and eagles slowed when they were a short

distance from the fortress, hovering again, watching as the unicorn riders reached the top of the mountain and entered the open gates.

The riders couldn't have been more than ten feet beyond the wall when the iron gates swung shut behind them, and Dynasian's voice rose over the clamor.

"Welcome riders," he said, parading across the ramparts. There was an oily quality to his voice that made Sheila's stomach turn. "Do not come any farther unless you wish to be directly responsible for your queen's death."

Sheila saw the riders shield their eyes against the glare of the sun as they followed the sound of Dynasian's voice: "I've been planning this little get-together for over a month now, and it pleases me greatly that you are so prompt.

"I have only one regret," the tyrant went on. "You are unable to see your queen, who took the more difficult route up the mountain. Were the sun not so bright, you would see she stands by my side. She is, I am afraid, a little disheartened. For she has just learned that the story that unicorns are held captive here is just that—a story. Further, she now realizes that she has led you all into a trap."

Nanine's contemptuous voice carried clearly. "He is insufferable!"

"I believe she owes you an apology." Dynasian shoved Illyria forward, perilously close to the edge of the ramparts. "Speak to them!" he ordered. "Tell them how you have betrayed them."

Illyria ignored the command, her face proud and calm.

"Do as he says, Lady." Nemor, who stood on her other side, spoke in a persuasive voice. "He does not like disobedience."

"Too late," Dynasian announced in a peevish tone.

"You're not following orders, Unicorn Queen." He turned to Nemor and uttered two succinct words: "Kill her."

Nemor hesitated just a moment. Horrified, Sheila screamed as Nemor stepped forward and pushed Illyria off the ramparts. Time seemed to stop as the Unicorn Queen plunged toward certain death.

Suddenly Quiet Storm moved with a speed that Sheila doubted a plane could equal. He swept down in front of the fortress beneath Illyria, catching her across his back as she fell.

Sheila hadn't even recovered from the surprise of it before Darian handed her his knife, telling her to cut the rope that bound Illyria's hands. Quiet Storm touched down lightly in the courtyard, and Darian and Sheila slipped from his back. Illyria remained on the unicorn's back, ready for the battle ahead.

Myno gave a loud, ringing cry, drew her sword—and then stopped dead in her tracks. The other riders also remained where they were, and Sheila knew why. The sun, now directly overhead, turned the fortress and its walls into a giant, glaring reflector, blinding anyone who stood in the courtyard. This was what Nemor had meant by natural defenses. They couldn't fight. They were sun-blind.

The riders shielded their eyes uselessly, unable to do anything but look at the ground. The wild part of the herd raced around them. Sheila wasn't sure whether or not the sun had the same effect on the unicorns. But there were no enemies for them to attack. The soldiers all stood safely on the walls, jeering at the helpless warriors below. Sheila knew it was only a matter of moments before the soldiers would begin picking the warriors off with well-placed arrows.

Suddenly a series of long dark shadows fell across the

fortress. A terrible high scream was heard. The soldiers looked up to see a formation of golden eagles circling the fortress. As the largest eagle cried out again, the flock dived for the men on the ramparts. They tore into the guards, knocking them from the walls, attacking until the ranks broke, panic-stricken.

There were the sounds of men running, swords being drawn, and the unicorns charging in a frenzy. Sheila had a feeling that more of Dynasian's reinforcements were pouring out of the fortress, but she couldn't be sure. All she could see was glare. *I've got to get out of this courtyard so I can see what's going on,* she told herself. She did the first thing she could think of—she took the pack from her back and held it to her forehead, using it as an oversized visor.

It took a moment to sort out what was going on. More soldiers, wearing visors on their helmets, had indeed rushed out and were heading for the riders. Both the eagles and unicorns were doing an impressive job of fighting the soldiers, but they were greatly outnumbered. Then the strangest combatant of all joined the fray. Pedaling like a madman on a ten-speed bicycle, and carrying a huge plastic garbage bag, Dr. Reit zoomed into the courtyard. The sun didn't bother him. He was wearing black Wayfarer sunglasses. He looked like an extra from *Miami Vice,* Sheila thought with astonishment.

Oblivious to the swords and arrows flashing through the air, Dr. Reit pedaled straight toward her. "There you are, dear girl!" he cried. "I've brought you supplies." He thrust the plastic garbage bag into Sheila's hand.

Sheila opened it and gave a loud whoop of laughter. The bag was filled with Ray-Ban sunglasses. Without missing a beat, she took a pair for herself and then dodged through the battle, distributing the sunglasses to the other riders and Laric's men, who, one by one, were changing into their human forms.

Dian actually smiled at Sheila as she put on her shades, but before Sheila could wonder about that, she found herself staring at the edge of a sword. And holding the sword was one of Dynasian's soldiers. Sheila couldn't make out the face beneath the helmet, but the man was at least six feet two, and from the arrogant way he moved, she could tell that he had marked her as easy prey.

Reflexively Sheila drew her own blade and blocked his first blow.

What am I doing? she wondered frantically as she dodged his next strike. *He's going to total me!*

She should have gone to the backpack instead of trying to fight with a weapon, but it was too late to change tactics now. This was one fight she would have to finish.

The soldier advanced with steady, deliberate blows. He didn't seem to be trying very hard to actually get through her guard, and with a sense of surprise, Sheila realized that he wasn't. He was simply going to wear her out. He would keep up his attack until she could no longer lift the sword against him.

Suddenly she heard Darian's words: "Easy . . . fight *your* fight," and understood that the soldier had been making her fight *his* fight—and he wasn't going to do it any longer.

His blade slashed down against her own, and then rose, preparing for the next swing. Sheila knew that he was counting on her to block it. So before his blade could complete its downward arc, she stepped in close and sliced the heavy leather armor open. The soldier looked at her in amazement, and, as he hesitated, she moved in again, taking the offense. He stumbled backward, trying to avoid her sword, and Sheila lost all fear. She went after the soldier with the sweet certainty of a victory, and only realized how thoroughly their roles had changed when he fled from her.

She was standing there feeling pleased with herself when a strong arm yanked her out of a spear's path. Darian pulled her against a wall, out of harm's way. "I told you you'd be a terror," he said with an approving grin. His grin faded as he looked straight ahead of them and caught sight of Dr. Reit. "What's he *doing*?" Darian asked.

Dr. Reit was, in fact, coming to Dian's rescue, though not in any way that Darian would have recognized. Having decided to run interference between Dian and an advancing soldier, the elderly scientist hunched down ("better aerodynamics," he would later explain) and rode over the amazed soldier's sandaled foot.

"Way to go, Dr. Reit!" Sheila cheered.

The scientist brought the bike to a rather jerky halt directly in front of her. "Yes, well . . ." he mumbled in his usual flustered tone. He looked around at the battle that was still raging. It was impossible to tell who was winning. "I realize this may not be the best time to exit," he began, "but I'm going to fade any second now. I can feel it."

"Okay," Sheila said, determined not to get all upset again. "Thanks for helping us. But how did you know to bring the sunglasses?"

"I told you I had to go back and investigate those 'natural defenses' Nemor mentioned," Dr. Reit explained. "It didn't take me long to figure out they were counting on the sun as their most powerful weapon. But let's get going. I'm starting to fade."

"What do you mean, 'let's'?" Sheila asked, confused. "Thanks for helping us. Come back when you can."

"You don't understand," Dr. Reit said. "This time you can fade with me. The bicycle will take us both."

Sheila couldn't believe what she was hearing. "You mean you're finally going to take me home?"

"Only if you get on the bike!" he shouted above the din. "There's not much time. Hurry!"

A lump rose in Sheila's throat. This was it. She was finally going home. It was what she had wanted ever since that crazy day when she fell into the time machine. Then why did she suddenly feel so sad? She scanned the courtyard, trying to get one last glimpse of each of her friends. Her eyes met Darian's and she had to look away.

"Sheila!" Dr. Reit's voice was weaker, and his image was wavering. "I can't stay much longer. You've got to get on *now!*"

"I know." Sheila brushed back a tear and reached for the bike—and at that moment she saw Illyria surrounded by three soldiers and fighting desperately for her life.

Before she had a chance to think about the consequences, she drew her sword and ran to Illyria's side. She and Darian each took on one of the soldiers. A jolt ran through her arm as she parried a blow meant for Illyria, giving the Unicorn Queen time to recover and fend off the first man. Laric, his sword moving with lightning speed, suddenly appeared and dispensed of the third soldier, who was matching blades with Darian. Sheila didn't mind at all when Laric then finished off her opponent.

Illyria finished her own fight, and Sheila breathed a sigh of relief. She turned back to where she had last seen Dr. Reit, but it was too late. The scientist was gone. How could she have let this happen? She had given up her only chance to go home. For the first time since the battle began, Sheila broke down and cried.

13

The Fortress

The rest of the battle passed in a blur. After helping Illyria, the only thing Sheila remembered clearly was the moment when Quiet Storm repaid Nemor for his treachery. The powerful unicorn had torn into the mercenary, goring and then trampling him as he lay wounded. The unicorns were all fierce, but Sheila had never seen anything this savage. Laric had said the lion and the unicorn could not meet without one of them dying. Quiet Storm gave Nemor no chance to survive.

A short time later it was over. The sun was beginning to set as the riders, the unicorns, and Laric's men stood grouped by the entrance to the fortress. Pelu was already applying bandages.

"Is everyone here?" Myno asked with a frown.

"Everyone except Dynasian," Nanine said darkly. "The pig has escaped."

"And the captive unicorns," Illyria added. She shook her head wearily. "They were never here. It was all a ruse to trap us. Dynasian spread the rumor throughout the countryside and I believed it."

"What happened to the Sareen?" Darian asked. "Weren't they supposed to ride up to the fortress with all of you?"

"Another lie. Nemor never told them about this," Illyria answered. "They didn't know he was a traitor, and I don't think he wanted them to find out. Maybe that was his saving grace—he could have sent them into the trap and didn't. Maybe he felt some responsibility to them after all."

Sheila stood listening, one arm around Morning Star's neck. She was exhausted and numb from all that had happened. She looked around at the group of riders, thinking, *This is my world now. This is as close as I'll come to family.* And then she realized that one very important member of the family wasn't there. "Illyria," she said, "Kara's missing."

The group fell quiet. They all knew where Kara was—somewhere inside the fortress, searching for Lianne.

"I'll find her," Sheila volunteered. She really didn't know why she said it, except she couldn't stand the idea of Kara in there alone searching for a sister who might not even be alive.

She patted Morning Star and walked toward the massive stone building. There were footsteps behind her, and she turned to see Darian.

"Thought I'd come along," he said as they stepped inside the building.

Together they walked through Dynasian's stronghold. For a building belonging to a man with such fussy taste, the inside of the fortress was surprisingly barren. Except for weapons on every wall, storerooms, and living quarters for the soldiers, there was little beyond empty, high-ceilinged hallways.

Their footsteps echoed in the hallways as they walked. There was no sign of Kara, Lianne, or any other slaves for that matter. Sheila was beginning to wonder if the story about Lianne was like the story of the captive unicorns—a lie designed to sweeten the bait.

At last they came to a passage that branched into another hallway. A woman's sobbing could be heard somewhere in the distance.

"There she is!" Sheila and Darian cried at once, each of them pointing in opposite directions.

They looked at each other with sheepish smiles. The inside of the fort was like a giant echo chamber. Either one of them could be right.

"I have an idea," said Darian. "Why don't I go in that direction—"

"And I'll go in this one," Sheila finished.

Darian nodded. "Look," he said, "I know you can take care of yourself, but be careful. Okay?"

"I will," Sheila promised. "You, too."

She turned and headed left, toward the sound of the sobbing. She was sure that she was getting closer. As she walked farther down the hall the sound became louder.

She kept going and soon realized it was fading. That meant that whoever was crying wasn't in the hallway but in a room off the hall, and she had passed it. Patiently she doubled back, this time trying every door she passed.

The doors were all locked—all except one. Sheila pushed against a low doorway, and it swung open into a small, dark room.

Cautiously she stepped inside and stopped. Kara knelt at the far end of the room, cradling a sobbing figure.

"You found her?" Sheila asked.

The archer looked up. It was too dark for Sheila to read her expression. "Yes, I've found her, but she's been badly frightened. She's been hiding in this room for weeks and doesn't want to leave. She's afraid the soldiers will hurt her. Maybe you can help me persuade her that it's safe to leave."

Sheila approached Lianne, a pretty, delicate girl who

looked to be about seventeen. In spite of the situation Sheila couldn't help making a snap judgment: Lianne would never make it as a rider. Almost at once she realized that anyone who had seen her on her first day in this world would have said the same thing about her. Remembering what it felt like to be scared and lost and confused, Sheila gently began to help coax the girl out of the room.

In the three weeks that Lianne had been hiding out, she had barely eaten. Kara and Sheila had to support her on either side for her to be able to walk, so leaving the fortress was a slow process. They had almost gotten Lianne to the main door when Darian found them. Sheila expected Lianne to be afraid of him, but Lianne gave Darian a shy smile and he immediately offered to help carry her.

Sheila stepped back and watched the trio move ahead. Lianne would heal, she thought, and like all the riders she would grow strong.

Kara, Lianne, and Darian opened the fortress door and stepped outside. Sheila was about to follow when suddenly the door slammed shut behind them. Sheila was alone in the fortress, and spinning wildly in the darkened hallway were the red lines of the *krino*. She had been right. Valan wasn't dead. He was here in the fortress with her.

Sheila felt strangely calm. Too much had happened that day for her to feel much more. She was simply wrung dry of all emotion. "What do you want?" she asked tonelessly.

The mage materialized at the sound of her voice. It occurred to her that she had given up her one chance to return home, and now Valan was going to kill her, and she was too exhausted to do anything about it. Some warrior she turned out to be.

"I seek only to make something clear to you, time traveler," he answered. "You and your friends have won today's battle. Despite my protection Nemor lies dead. But despite your sorcerer friend and your own magic"—he indicated her backpack—"you will not win. And you will all pay for Nemor's death." He spoke in the voice of prophecy, and Sheila felt herself grow cold as he continued. "Laric and his men will soon remain eagles never to transform, and the unicorns will be destroyed."

Believe him and you fight his fight, Sheila told herself.

She shrugged and made her voice as sure and steady as she could. "You've been stopped before. You can be stopped again."

"Let me show you, then, what you're really up against," said Valan softly. The *krino* began to spin furiously. Sheila reached toward her pack for the mirror, knowing that she didn't have time to find it, much less use it.

But this time Valan did not use the *krino* as a weapon. Instead, the glowing red light spun around his own form, weaving a network of fine red lines that shimmered in the darkness, completely covering his figure.

There was a hissing sound, and then Valan was gone. Sheila gasped and took a step back. As the red of the *krino* faded she saw him—Mardock. Mardock, with his long, black curls and elegant silk robe. Mardock, whose magic drew the Dark Gods' power to Dynasian.

"Valan," he explained smoothly, "was just an amusing game I chose to play with you. But I was not pleased with the outcome of that game. When my wounds have healed, I am the one you will deal with, Sheila McCarthy. Do not forget that."

Sheila saw that his face was marred by a deep red welt. *The mirror,* she thought. *It burned him.*

And then as suddenly as he had appeared Mardock was gone. Sheila was truly alone in the fortress with only her fear and silence echoing through the empty halls. It took her a moment to collect herself and then Sheila flung the door open and ran—straight into Illyria and Laric.

The Unicorn Queen caught her, placing her hands on Sheila's shoulders. "What's the hurry? Are you all right?"

"I'm fine," Sheila answered, "but I just ran into Valan . . . I mean, Mardock . . ."

"All the better," said Laric when she had finished. "Then there is only one mage I must destroy." He didn't look at all intimidated by Mardock's threats. Actually, he had his arm around Illyria and was looking extremely romantic.

"I came looking for you because I wanted to thank you," Illyria said, not even addressing the question of Mardock. "Darian told me what you did—that you gave up the chance to return to your home in order to save my life."

Sheila didn't know what to say.

"I know that wasn't easy," Illyria went on. "You come from a different time and world, and yet you have proved yourself the equal of my best warriors." The Unicorn Queen smiled. "A fighter who doesn't like to fight—you have great courage, Sheila McCarthy. I want you to know that for as long as you remain in this world, you have a home with us."

Sheila said the only thing she could. "Thank you." But she had never felt prouder.

Myno barked an order to prepare to ride. Smiling, Sheila called to Morning Star and lifted herself into the saddle. Feeling tired, but strong and happy, she joined the other unicorn warriors and rode out to adventure beneath the rising moon.

SECRET THE OF THE
Unicorn Queen

Once again, the Unicorn Queen's warriors are victorious! Yet there are still more unicorns to free, so the group must head back towards Dynasian's palace.

But besides that task, Laric and his men must be freed from the evil spell that Dynasian cast upon them. Sheila's bravery is again put to the test, as she sneaks into Dynasian's laboratory to try and steal the formula for the antidote. Can Sheila do this without getting caught? And if she is successful, is there someone who can prepare the antidote? But most important, will Sheila ever get home??

Find out all the answers as the excitement continues in

THE SECRET OF THE UNICORN QUEEN #3:

THE FINAL TEST